Women's Slave Narratives

Annie L. Burton
and Others

DOVER PUBLICATIONS, INC.
Mineola, New York

Bibliographical Note

This Dover edition, first published in 2006, consists of a slightly abridged republication of *Memories of Childhood's Slavery Days*, Ross Publishing Company, Boston, 1909, as well as the unabridged republication of *Memoir of Old Elizabeth, A Coloured Woman*, Collins Printer, Philadelphia, 1863; *The Story of Mattie J. Jackson*, Sentinel Office, Lawrence, Massachusetts, 1866; *From the Darkness Cometh the Light, or Struggles for Freedom*, J. T. Smith Publishing House, St. Louis, Missouri, c. 1891; and *A Slave Girl's Story*, Brooklyn, New York, 1898.

Library of Congress Cataloging-in-Publication Data

Women's slave narratives / Annie L. Burton . . . [et al.]
    p. cm.
    Contents: Memories of childhood's slavery days / Annie L. Burton—Memoir of old Elizabeth, a coloured woman— The story of Mattie J. Jackson—From the darkness cometh the light, or Struggles for freedom / Lucy A. Delaney—A slave girl's story / Kate Drumgoold.
    ISBN 0-486-44555-0 (pbk.)
    1. Women slaves—United States—Biography. 2. Slaves—United States—Biography. 3. Slaves' writings, American. I. Burton, Annie L., b. 1858?

E444.W8 2006
306.3'62'092273—dc22

2005051791

Manufactured in the United States of America
Dover Publications, Inc., 31 East 2nd Street, Mineola, N.Y. 11501

Contents

Memories of Childhood's Slavery Days

Memories of Childhood's Slavery Days

Annie L. Burton

RECOLLECTIONS OF A HAPPY LIFE

The memory of my happy, care-free childhood days on the plantation, with my little white and black companions, is often with me. Neither master nor mistress nor neighbors had time to bestow a thought upon us, for the great Civil War was raging. That great event in American history was a matter wholly outside the realm of our childish interests. Of course we heard our elders discuss the various events of the great struggle, but it meant nothing to us.

On the plantation there were ten white children and fourteen colored children. Our days were spent roaming about from plantation to plantation, not knowing or caring what things were going on in the great world outside our little realm. Planting time and harvest time were happy days for us. How often at the harvest time the planters discovered cornstalks missing from the ends of the rows, and blamed the crows! We were called the "little fairy devils." To the sweet potatoes and peanuts and sugar cane we also helped ourselves.

Those slaves that were not married served the food from the great house, and about half-past eleven they would send the older children with food to the workers in the fields. Of course, I followed, and before we got to the fields, we had eaten the food nearly all up. When the workers returned home they complained, and we were whipped.

The slaves got their allowance every Monday night of molasses, meat, corn meal, and a kind of flour called "dredgings" or "shorts." Perhaps this allowance would be gone before the next Monday night, in which case the slaves would steal hogs and chickens. Then would come the whipping-post. Master himself never whipped his slaves; this was left to the overseer.

We children had no supper, and only a little piece of bread or something of the kind in the morning. Our dishes consisted of one wooden bowl, and oyster shells were our spoons. This bowl served for about fifteen children, and often the dogs and the ducks and the peafowl had a dip in it. Sometimes we had buttermilk and bread in our bowl, sometimes greens or bones.

Our clothes were little homespun cotton slips, with short sleeves. I never knew what shoes were until I got big enough to earn them myself.

If a slave man and woman wished to marry, a party would be arranged some Saturday night among the slaves. The marriage ceremony consisted of the pair jumping over a stick. If no children were born within a year or so, the wife was sold.

At New Year's, if there was any debt or mortgage on the plantation, the extra slaves were taken to Clayton and sold at the court house. In this way families were separated.

When they were getting recruits for the war, we were allowed to go to Clayton to see the soldiers.

I remember, at the beginning of the war, two colored men were hung in Clayton; one, Caesar King, for killing a blood hound and biting off an overseer's ear; the other, Dabney Madison, for the murder of his master. Dabney Madison's master was really shot by a man named Houston, who was infatuated with Madison's mistress, and who had hired Madison to make the bullets for him. Houston escaped after the deed, and the blame fell on Dabney Madison, as he was the only slave of his master and mistress. The clothes of the two victims were hung on two pine trees, and no colored person would touch them. Since I have grown up, I have seen the skeleton of one of these men in the office of a doctor in Clayton.

After the men were hung, the bones were put in an old deserted house. Somebody that cared for the bones used to put them in the sun in bright weather, and back in the house when it rained. Finally the bones disappeared, although the boxes that had contained them still remained.

At one time, when they were building barns on the plantation, one of the big boys got a little brandy and gave us children all a drink, enough to make us drunk. Four doctors were sent for, but nobody could tell what was the matter with us, except they thought we had eaten something poisonous. They wanted to give us some castor oil, but we refused to take it, because we thought that the oil was made from the bones of the dead men we had seen. Finally, we told about the big white boy giving us the brandy, and the mystery was cleared up.

Young as I was then, I remember this conversation between master and mistress, on master's return from the gate one day, when he had received the latest news: "William, what is the news from the seat of war?" "A great battle was fought at Bull Run, and the Confederates won," he replied. "Oh, good, good," said mistress, "and what did Jeff Davis say?" "Look out for the blockade. I do not know what the end may be soon," he answered. "What does Jeff Davis mean by that?" she asked. "Sarah Anne, I don't know, unless he means that the niggers will be free." "O, my God, what shall we do?" "I presume," he said, "we shall have to put our boys to work and hire help." "But," she said, "what will the niggers do if they are free? Why, they will starve if we don't keep them." "Oh, well," he said, "let them wander, if they will not stay with their owners. I don't doubt that many owners have been good to their slaves, and they would rather remain with their owners than wander about without home or country."

My mistress often told me that my father was a planter who owned a plantation about two miles from ours. He was a white man, born in Liverpool, England. He died in Lewisville, Alabama, in the year 1875.

I will venture to say that I only saw my father a dozen times, when I was about four years old; and those times I saw him only from a distance, as he was driving by the great house of our plantation. Whenever my mistress saw him going by, she would take me by the hand and run out upon the piazza, and exclaim, "Stop there, I say! Don't you want to see and speak to and caress your darling child? She often speaks of you and wants to embrace her dear father. See what a bright and beautiful daughter she is, a perfect picture of yourself. Well, I declare, you are an affectionate father." I well remember that whenever my mistress would speak thus and upbraid him, he would whip up his horse and get out of sight and hearing as quickly as possible. My mistress's action was, of course, intended to humble and shame my father. I never spoke to him, and cannot remember that he ever noticed me, or in any way acknowledged me to be his child.

My mother and my mistress were children together, and grew up to be mothers together. My mother was the cook in my mistress's household. One morning when master had gone to Eufaula, my mother and my mistress got into an argument, the consequence of which was that my mother was whipped, for the first time in her life. Whereupon, my mother refused to do any more work, and ran away from the plantation. For three years we did not see her again.

Our plantation was one of several thousand acres, comprising large level fields, upland, and considerable forests of Southern pine. Cotton, corn, sweet potatoes, sugar cane, wheat, and rye were the principal crops raised on the plantation. It was situated near the P——— River, and about twenty-three miles from Clayton, Ala.

One day my master heard that the Yankees were coming our way, and he immediately made preparations to get his goods and valuables out of their reach. The big six-mule team was brought to the smoke-house door, and loaded with hams and provisions. After being loaded, the team was put in the care of two of the most trustworthy and valuable slaves that my master owned, and driven away. It was master's intention to have these things taken to a swamp, and there concealed in a pit that had recently been made for the purpose. But just before the team left the main road for the by-road that led to the swamp, the two slaves were surprised by the Yankees, who at once took possession of the provisions, and started the team toward Clayton, where the

Yankees had headquarters. The road to Clayton ran past our plantation. One of the slave children happened to look up the road, and saw the Yankees coming, and gave warning. Whereupon, my master left unceremoniously for the woods, and remained concealed there for five days. The niggers had run away whenever they got a chance, but now it was master's and the other white folks' turn to run.

The Yankees rode up to the piazza of the great house and inquired who owned the plantation. They gave orders that nothing must be touched or taken away, as they intended to return shortly and take possession. My mistress and the slaves watched for their return day and night for more than a week, but the Yankees did not come back.

One morning in April, 1865, my master got the news that the Yankees had left Mobile Bay and crossed the Confederate lines, and that the Emancipation Proclamation had been signed by President Lincoln. Mistress suggested that the slaves should not be told of their freedom; but master said he would tell them, because they would soon find it out, even if he did not tell them. Mistress, however, said she could keep my mother's three children, for my mother had now been gone so long.

All the slaves left the plantation upon the news of their freedom, except those who were feeble or sickly. With the help of these, the crops were gathered. My mistress and her daughters had to go to the kitchen and to the washtub. My little half-brother, Henry, and myself had to gather chips, and help all we could. My sister, Caroline, who was twelve years old, could help in the kitchen.

After the war, the Yankees took all the good mules and horses from the plantation, and left their old army stock. We children chanced to come across one of the Yankees' old horses, that had "U.S." branded on him. We called him "Old Yank" and got him fattened up. One day in August, six of us children took "Old Yank" and went away back on the plantation for watermelons. Coming home, we thought we would make the old horse trot. When "Old Yank" commenced to trot, our big melons dropped off, but we couldn't stop the horse for some time. Finally, one of the big boys went back and got some more melons, and left us eating what we could find of the ones that had been dropped. Then all we six, with our melons, got on "Old Yank" and went home. We also used to hitch "Old Yank" into a wagon and get wood. But one sad day in the fall, the Yankees came back again, and gathered up their old stock, and took "Old Yank" away.

One day mistress sent me out to do some churning under a tree. I went to sleep and jerked the churn over on top of me, and consequently got a whipping.

My mother came for us at the end of the year 1865, and demanded that her children be given up to her. This, mistress refused to do, and threatened to set the dogs on my mother if she did not at once leave the place. My mother went away, and remained with some of the neighbors until supper time. Then she got a boy to tell Caroline to come down to the fence. When she came, my mother told her to go back and get Henry and myself and bring us down to the gap in the fence as quick as she could. Then my mother took Henry in her arms, and my sister carried me on her back. We climbed fences and crossed fields, and after several hours came to a little hut which my mother had secured on a plantation. We had no more than reached the place, and made a little fire, when master's two sons rode up and demanded that the children be returned. My mother refused to give us up. Upon her offering to go with them to the Yankee headquarters to find out if it were really true that all negroes had been made free, the young men left, and troubled us no more.

The cabin that was now our home was made of logs. It had one door, and an opening in one wall, with an inside shutter, was the only window. The door was fastened with a latch. Our beds were some straw.

There were six in our little family; my mother, Caroline, Henry, two other children that my mother had brought with her upon her return, and myself.

The man on whose plantation this cabin stood, hired my mother as cook, and gave us this little home. We children used to sell blueberries and plums that we picked. One day the man on whom we depended for our home and support, left. Then my mother did washing by the day, for whatever she could get. We were sent to get cold victuals from hotels and such places. A man wanting hands to pick cotton, my brother Henry and I were set to help in this work. We had to go to the cotton field very early every morning. For this work, we received forty cents for every hundred pounds of cotton we picked.

Caroline was hired out to take care of a baby.

In 1866, another man hired the plantation on which our hut stood, and we moved into Clayton, to a little house my mother secured there. A rich lady came to our house one day, looking for some one to take care of her little daughter. I was taken, and adopted into this family. This rich lady was Mrs. E. M. Williams, a music teacher, the wife of a lawyer. We called her "Mis' Mary."

Some rich people in Clayton who had owned slaves, opened the Methodist church on Sundays, and began the work of teaching the negroes. My new mistress sent me to Sunday school every Sunday morning, and I soon got so that I could read. Mis' Mary taught me every day at her knee. I soon could read nicely, and went through Sterling's Second Reader, and then into McGuthrie's Third Reader. The first piece of poetry I recited in Sunday school was taught to me by Mis' Mary during the week. Mis' Mary's father-in-law, an ex-judge, of Clayton, Alabama, heard me recite it, and thought it was wonderful. It was this.

"I am glad to see you, little bird,
It was your sweet song I heard.
What was it I heard you say?
Give me crumbs to eat today?
Here are crumbs I brought for you.
Eat your dinner, eat away,
Come and see us every day."

After this Mis' Mary kept on with my studies, and taught me to write. As I grew older, she taught me to cook and how to do housework. During this time Mis' Mary had given my mother one dollar a month in return for my services; now as I grew up to young womanhood, I thought I would like a little money of my own. Accordingly, Mis' Mary began to pay me four dollars a month, besides giving me my board and clothes. For two summers she "let me out" while she was away, and I got five dollars a month.

While I was with Mis' Mary, I had my first sweetheart, one of the young fellows who attended Sunday school with me. Mis' Mary, however, objected to the young man's coming to the house to call, because she did not think I was old enough to have a sweetheart.

I owe a great deal to Mis' Mary for her good training of me, in honesty, uprightness and truthfulness. She told me that when I went out into the world all white folks would not treat me as she had, but that I must not feel bad about it, but just do what I was employed to do, and if I wasn't satisfied, to go elsewhere; but always to carry an honest name.

One Sunday when my sweetheart walked to the gate with me, Mis' Mary met him and told him she thought I was too young for him, and that she was sending me to Sunday school to learn, not to catch a beau. It was a long while before he could see me again,—not until later in the season, in watermelon time, when Mis' Mary and my mother gave me permission to go to a watermelon party one Sunday afternoon. Mis' Mary did not know, however, that my sweetheart had planned to escort me. We met around the corner of the house, and after the party he left me at the same place. After that I saw him occasionally at barbecues and parties. I was permitted to go with him some evenings to church, but my mother always walked ahead or behind me and the young man.

We went together for four years. During that time, although I still called Mis' Mary's my home, I had been out to service in one or two families.

Finally, my mother and Mis' Mary consented to our marriage, and the wedding day was to be in May. The winter before that May, I went to service in the family of Dr. Drury in Eufaula. Just a week before I left Clayton I dreamed that my sweetheart died suddenly. The night before I was to leave, we were invited out to tea. He told me he had bought a nice piece of poplar wood, with which to make a table for our new home. When I told him my dream, he said, "Don't let that trouble you, there is nothing in dreams." But one month from that day he died, and his coffin was made from the piece of poplar wood he had bought for the table.

After his death, I remained in Clayton for two or three weeks with my people, and then went back to Eufaula, where I stayed two years.

My sweetheart's death made a profound impression on me, and I began to pray as best I could. Often I remained all night on my knees.

Going on an excursion to Macon, Georgia, one time, I liked the place so well that I did not go back to Eufaula. I got a place as cook in the family of an Episcopal clergyman, and remained with them eight years, leaving when the family moved to New Orleans.

During these eight years, my mother died in Clayton, and I had to take the three smallest children into my care. My oldest sister was now married, and had a son.

I now went to live with a Mrs. Maria Campbell, a colored woman, who adopted me and gave me her name. Mrs. Campbell did washing and ironing for her living. While living with her, I went six months to Lewis' High School in Macon. Then I went to Atlanta, and obtained a place as first-class cook with Mr. E. N. Inman. But I always considered Mrs. Campbell's my home. I remained about a year with Mr. Inman, and received as wages ten dollars a month.

One day, when the family were visiting in Memphis, I chanced to pick up a newspaper, and read the advertisement of a Northern family for a cook to go to Boston. I went at once to the address given, and made agreement to take the place, but told the people that I could not leave my present position until Mr. Inman returned home. Mr. and Mrs. Inman did not want to let me go, but I made up my mind to go North. The Northern family whose service I was to enter had returned to Boston before I left, and had made arrangements with a friend, Mr. Bullock, to see me safely started North.

After deciding to go North, I went to Macon, to make arrangements with Mrs. Campbell for the care of my two sisters who lived with her. One sister was now about thirteen and the other fifteen, both old enough to do a little for themselves. My brother was dead. He went to Brunswick in 1875, and died there of the yellow fever in 1876. One sister I brought in later years to Boston. I stayed in Macon two weeks, and was in Atlanta three or four days before leaving for the North.

About the 15th of June, 1879, I arrived at the Old Colony Station in Boston, and had my first glimpse of the country I had heard so much about. From Boston I went to Newtonville, where I was to work. The gentleman whose service I was to enter, Mr. E. N. Kimball, was waiting at the station for me, and drove me to his home on Warner Street. For a few days, until I got somewhat adjusted to my new circumstances, I had no work to do. On June 17th the family took me with them to Auburndale. But in spite of the kindness of Mrs. Kimball and the colored nurse, I grew very homesick for the South, and would often look in the direction of my old home and cry.

The washing, a kind of work I knew nothing about, was given to me; but I could not do it, and it was finally given over to a hired woman. I had to do the ironing of the fancy clothing for Mrs. Kimball and the children.

About five or six weeks after my arrival, Mrs. Kimball and the children went to the White Mountains for the summer, and I had more leisure. Mr. Kimball went up to the mountains every Saturday night, to stay with his family over Sunday; but he and his father-in-law were at home other nights, and I had to have dinner for them.

To keep away the homesickness and loneliness as much as possible, I made acquaintance with the hired girl across the street.

One morning I climbed up into the cherry tree that grew between Mr. Kimball's yard and the yard of his next-door neighbor, Mr. Roberts. I was thinking of the South, and as I picked the cherries, I sang a Southern song. Mr. Roberts heard me, and gave me a dollar for the song.

By agreement, Mrs. Kimball was to give me three dollars and a half a week, instead of four, until the difference amounted to my fare from the South; after that, I was to have four dollars. I had, however, received but little money. In the fall, after the family came home, we had a little difficulty about my wages, and I left and came into Boston. One of my Macon acquaintances had come North before me, and now had a position as cook in a

house on Columbus Avenue. I looked this girl up. Then I went
to a lodging-house for colored people on Kendall Street, and
spent one night there. Mrs. Kimball had refused to give me a
recommendation, because she wanted me to stay with her, and
thought the lack of a recommendation would be an inducement.
In the lodging-house I made acquaintance with a colored girl,
who took me to an intelligence office. The man at the desk said
he would give me a card to take to 24 Springfield Street, on
receipt of fifty cents. I had never heard of an office of this kind,
and asked a good many questions. After being assured that my
money would be returned in case I did not accept the situation,
I paid the fifty cents and started to find the address on the card.
Being ignorant of the scheme of street numbering, I inquired of
a woman whom I met, where No. 24 was. This woman asked me
if I was looking for work, and when I told her I was, she said a
friend of hers on Springfield Street wanted a servant immediately. Of course I went with this lady, and after a conference
with the mistress of the house as to my ability, when I could
begin work, what wages I should want, etc., I was engaged as
cook at three dollars and a half a week.

From this place I proceeded to 24 Springfield Street, as
directed, hoping that I would be refused, so that I might go back
to the intelligence office and get my fifty cents. The lady at No.
24 who wanted a servant, said she didn't think I was large and
strong enough, and guessed I wouldn't do. Then I went and got
my fifty cents.

Having now obtained a situation, I sent to Mr. Kimball's for
my trunk. I remained in my new place a year and a half. At the
end of that time the family moved to Dorchester, and because I
did not care to go out there, I left their service.

From this place, I went to Narragansett Pier to work as a
chambermaid for the summer. In the fall, I came back to Boston
and obtained a situation with a family, in Berwick Park. This
family afterward moved to Jamaica Plain, and I went with them.
With this family I remained seven years. They were very kind to
me, gave me two or three weeks' vacation, without loss of pay.

In June, 1884, I went with them to their summer home in the
Isles of Shoals, as housekeeper for some guests who were com-

ing from Paris. On the 6th of July I received word that my sister Caroline had died in June. This was a great blow to me. I remained with the Reeds until they closed their summer home, but I was not able to do much work after the news of my sister's death.

I wrote home to Georgia, to the white people who owned the house in which Caroline had lived, asking them to take care of her boy Lawrence until I should come in October. When we came back to Jamaica Plain in the fall, I was asked to decide what I should do in regard to this boy. Mrs. Reed wanted me to stay with her, and promised to help pay for the care of the boy in Georgia. Of course, she said, I could not expect to find positions if I had a child with me. As an inducement to remain in my present place and leave the boy in Georgia, I was promised provision for my future days, as long as I should live. It did not take me long to decide what I should do. The last time I had seen my sister, a little over a year before she died, she had said, when I was leaving, "I don't expect ever to see you again, but if I die I shall rest peacefully in my grave, because I know you will take care of my child."

I left Jamaica Plain and took a room on Village Street for the two or three weeks until my departure for the South. During this time, a lady came to the house to hire a girl for her home in Wellesley Hills. The girl who was offered the place would not go. I volunteered to accept the position temporarily, and went at once to the beautiful farm. At the end of a week, a man and his wife had been engaged, and I was to leave the day after their arrival. These new servants, however, spoke very little English, and I had to stay through the next week until the new ones were broken in. After leaving there I started for Georgia, reaching there at the end of five days, at five o'clock.

I took a carriage and drove at once to the house where Lawrence was being taken care of. He was playing in the yard, and when he saw me leave the carriage he ran and threw his arms around my neck and cried for joy. I stayed a week in this house, looking after such things of my sister's as had not been already stored. One day I had a headache, and was lying down in the cook's room. Lawrence was in the dining-room with the cook's little girl, and the two got into a quarrel, in the course of which my nephew struck the cook's child. The cook, in her anger, chased the boy with a broom, and threatened to give him a good whipping at all costs. Hearing the noise, I came out into the yard, and when Lawrence saw me he ran to me for protection. I interceded for him, and promised he should get into no more trouble. We went at once to a neighbor's house for the night. The next day I got a room in the yard of a house belonging to some white people. Here we stayed two weeks. The only return I was asked to make for the room was to weed the garden. Lawrence and I dug out some weeds and burned them, but came so near setting fire to the place that we were told we need not dig any more weeds, but that we might have the use of the room so long as we cared to stay.

In about a week and a half more we got together such things as we wanted to keep and take away with us.

The last time I saw my sister, I had persuaded her to open a bank account, and she had done so, and had made small deposits from time to time. When I came to look for the bankbook, I discovered that her lodger, one Mayfield, had taken it at her death, and nobody knew where it might be now. I found out that Mayfield had drawn thirty dollars from the account for my sister's burial, and also an unknown amount for himself. He had done nothing for the boy. I went down to the bank, and was told that Mayfield claimed to look after my sister's burial and her affairs. He had made one Reuben Bennett, who was no relation and had no interest in the matter, administrator for Lawrence, until his coming of age. But Bennett had as yet done nothing for him. The book was in the bank, with some of the account still undrawn, how much I did not know. I next went to see a lawyer, to find out how much it would cost me to get this book. The lawyer said fifteen dollars. I said I would call again. In the meantime, I went to the court house, and when the case on trial was adjourned I went to the judge and stated my case. The judge, who was slightly acquainted with my sister and me, told me to have Reuben Bennett in court next morning at nine o'clock, and to bring Lawrence with me. When we had all assembled before the judge, he told Bennett to take Lawrence and go to the bank

and get the money belonging to my sister. Bennett went and collected the money, some thirty-five dollars. The boy was then
given into my care by the judge. For his kindness, the judge
would accept no return. Happy at having obtained the money so
easily, we went back to our room, and rested until our departure
the next night for Jacksonville, Florida. I had decided to go to
this place for the winter, on account of Lawrence, thinking the
Northern winter would be too severe for him.

My youngest sister, who had come to Macon from Atlanta a
few days before my arrival, did not hear of Caroline's death until
within a few days of our departure. This youngest sister decided
to go to Florida with us for the winter.

Our trunks and baggage were taken to the station in a team.
We had a goodly supply of food, given us by our friends and by
the people whose hospitality we had shared during the latter
part of our stay.

The next morning we got into Jacksonville. My idea was to get
a place as chambermaid at Green Cove Springs, Florida,
through the influence of the head waiter at a hotel there, whom
I knew. After I got into Jacksonville I changed my plans. I did
not see how I could move my things any farther, and we went to
a hotel for colored people, hired a room for two dollars, and
boarded ourselves on the food which had been given us in
Macon. This food lasted about two weeks. Then I had to buy,
and my money was going every day, and none coming in, I did
not know what to do. One night the idea of keeping a restaurant
came to me, and I decided to get a little home for the three of
us, and then see what I could do in this line of business. After a
long and hard search, I found a little house of two rooms where
we could live, and the next day I found a place to start my
restaurant. For house furnishings, we used at first, to the best
advantage we could, the things we had brought from Macon.
Caroline's cookstove had been left with my foster-mother in
Macon. After hiring the room for the restaurant, I sent for this
stove, and it arrived in a few days. Then I went to a dealer in sec-
ond-hand furniture and got such things as were actually needed
for the house and the restaurant, on the condition that he would
take them back at a discount when I got through with them.

Trade at the restaurant was very good, and we got along nicely. My sister got a position as nurse for fifteen dollars a month. One day the cook from a shipwrecked vessel came to my restaurant, and in return for his board and a bed in the place, agreed to do my cooking. After trade became good, I changed my residence to a house of four rooms, and put three cheap cots in each of two of the rooms, and let the cots at a dollar a week apiece to colored men who worked nearby in hotels. Lawrence and I did the chamber work at night, after the day's work in the restaurant.

I introduced "Boston baked beans" into my restaurant, much to the amusement of the people at first; but after they had once eaten them it was hard to meet the demand for beans.

Lawrence, who was now about eleven years old, was a great help to me. He took out dinners to the cigarmakers in a factory nearby.

At the end of the season, about four months, it had grown so hot that we could stay in Jacksonville no longer. From my restaurant and my lodgers I cleared one hundred and seventy-five dollars, which I put into the Jacksonville bank. Then I took the furniture back to the dealer, who fulfilled his agreement.

My sister decided to go back to Atlanta when she got through with her place as nurse, which would not be for some weeks.

I took seventy-five dollars out of my bank account, and with Lawrence went to Fernandina. There we took train to Port Royal, S. C., then steamer to New York. From New York we went to Brooklyn for a few days. Then we went to Newport and stayed with a woman who kept a lodging-house. I decided to see what I could do in Newport by keeping a boarding and lodging-house. I hired a little house and agreed to pay nine dollars a month for it. I left Lawrence with some neighbors while I came to Boston and took some things out of storage. These things I moved into the little house. But I found, after paying one month's rent, that the house was not properly located for the business I wanted. I left, and with Lawrence went to Narragansett Pier. I got a place there as "runner" for a laundry; that is, I was to go to the hotels and leave cards and solicit trade. Then Lawrence thought he would like to help by doing a little work. One night when I came back from the laundry, I missed him. Nobody had seen him. All night I searched for him, but did not find him. In the early morning I met him coming home. He said a man who kept a bowling alley had hired him at fifty cents a week to set up the pins, and it was in the bowling alley he had been all night. He said the man let him take a nap on his coat when he got sleepy. I went at once to see this man, and told him not to hire my nephew again. A lady who kept a hotel offered me two dollars a week for Lawrence's services in helping the cook and serving in the help's dining-room. When the season closed, the lady who hired Lawrence was very reluctant to let him go.

We went back to Newport to see the landlady from whom I had hired the house, and I paid such part of the rent as I could. Then I packed my things and started for Boston. On reaching there, I kept such of my things as I needed, and stored the rest, and took a furnished room. In about a week's time I went to see the husband of the lady for whom I had worked at Wellesley Hills just previous to my departure for the South. He had told me to let him know when I returned to Boston. He said a man and his wife were at present employed at his farm, but he didn't know how long they would stay. Before another week had passed, this gentleman sent for me. He said his wife wanted me to go out to the farm, and that I could have Lawrence with me. The boy, he said, could help his wife with the poultry, and could have a chance to go to school. I was promised three dollars and a half a week, and no washing to do. I was told that the farm had been offered for sale, and of course it might change hands any day. I was promised, however, that I should lose nothing by the change.

Lawrence was very lonely at the farm, with no companions, and used to sit and cry.

The place was sold about ten weeks after I went there, and I came into Boston to look about for a restaurant, leaving Lawrence at the farm. When the home was broken up, the owners came to the Revere House, Boston. Barrels of apples, potatoes and other provisions were given to me.

I found a little restaurant near the Providence depot for sale. I made arrangements at once to buy the place for thirty-five dollars, and the next day I brought Lawrence and my things from

Wellesley Hills. I paid two dollars a week rent for my little restaurant, and did very well. The next spring I sold the place for fifty dollars, in time to get a place at the beach for the summer. Lawrence got a position in a drug store, and kept it four years. Then he went to Hampton College, Hampton, Va. After finishing there, he came back and then went to the World's Fair in Chicago. After that he took a position on one of the Fall River line boats. At the outbreak of the Spanish War, he enlisted in Brooklyn as powderman on the battleship Texas. He was on the Texas when the first shot was fired. He was present at the decoration of the graves of the American soldiers in Havana, and also at the decoration of the battleship Maine after she was raised. After the war, he came to Brooklyn and got an honorable discharge. Then he served as valet to a rich New York man, who travelled a good deal. About the middle of last November (1906) Lawrence came to Boston to see me. He is now in Atlantic City, a waiter in the Royal Hotel.

In 1888, I was married, at 27 Pemberton Street, to Samuel H. Burton, by Dr. O. P. Gifford. After my marriage, Mr. Burton got a place in Braintree as valet to an old gentleman who was slightly demented, and he could not be satisfied until I joined him. So I put our things into storage and went to Braintree. I remained there ten months, and then came back to Boston. Then I got a position as head matron in the help's dining-room in a hotel at Watch Hill, R. I. My husband was also there as waiter. At the end of the season we both came home, and rented a lodging-house, and lost money on it.

REMINISCENCES

The times changed from slavery days to freedom's days. As young as I was, my thoughts were mystified to see such wonderful changes; yet I did not know the meaning of these changing days. But days glided by, and in my mystified way I could see and hear many strange things. I would see my master and mistress in close conversation and they seemed anxious about something that I, a child, could not know the meaning of.

But as weeks went by, I began to understand. I saw all the slaves one by one disappearing from the plantation (for night and day they kept going) until there was not one to be seen.

All around the plantation was left barren. Day after day I could run down to the gate and see down the road troops and troops of Garrison's Brigade, and in the midst of them gangs and gangs of negro slaves who joined with the soldiers, shouting, dancing and clapping their hands. The war was ended, and from Mobile Bay to Clayton, Ala., all along the road, on all the plantations, the slaves thought that if they joined the Yankee soldiers they would be perfectly safe.

As I looked on these I did not know what it meant, for I had never seen such a circus. The Yankee soldiers found that they had such an army of men and women and children, that they had to build tents and feed them to keep them from starving. But from what I, a little child, saw and heard the older ones say, that must have been a terrible time of trouble. I heard my master and mistress talking. They said, "Well, I guess those Yankees had such a large family on their hands, we rather guessed those fanatics on freedom would be only too glad to send some back for their old masters to provide for them."

But they never came back to our plantation, and I could only speak of my own home, but I thought to myself, what would become of my good times all over the old plantation. Oh, the harvesting times, the great hog-killing times when several hundred hogs were killed, and we children watched and got our share of the slaughter in pig's liver roasted on a bed of coals, eaten ashes and all. Then came the great sugar-cane grinding time, when they were making the molasses, and we children would be hanging round, drinking the sugar-cane juice, and awaiting the moment to help ourselves to everything good. We did, too, making ourselves sticky and dirty with the sweet stuff being made. Not only were the slave children there, but the little white children from Massa's house would join us and have a jolly time. The negro child and the white child knew not the great chasm between their lives, only that they had dainties and we had crusts.

My sister, being the children's nurse, would take them and

wash their hands and put them to bed in their luxurious bed-rooms, while we little slaves would find what homes we could. My brother and I would go to sleep on some lumber under the house, where our sister Caroline would find us and put us to bed. She would wipe our hands and faces and make up our beds on the floor in Massa's house, for we had lived with him ever since our own mother had run away, after being whipped by her mistress. Later on, after the war, my mother returned and claimed us. I never knew my father, who was a white man.

During these changing times, just after the war, I was trying to find out what the change would bring about for us, as we were under the care of our mistress, living in the great house. I thought this: that Henry, Caroline and myself, Louise, would have to go as others had done, and where should we go and what should we do? But as time went on there were many changes. Our mistress and her two daughters, Martha and Mary, had to become their own servants, and do all the work of the house, going into the kitchen, cooking and washing, and feeling very angry that all their house servants had run away to the Yankees. The time had come when our good times were over, our many leisure hours spent among the cotton fields and woods and our half-holiday on Saturday. These were all gone. The boys had to leave school and take the runaway slaves' places to finish the planting and pick the cotton. I myself have worked in the cotton field, picking great baskets full, too heavy for me to carry. All was over! I now fully understood the change in our circumstances. Little Henry and I had no more time to sit basking ourselves in the sunshine of the sunny south. The land was empty and the servants all gone. I can see my dainty mistress coming down the steps saying, "Rit, you and Henry will have to go and pick up some chips, for Miss Mary and myself have to prepare the breakfast. You children will have to learn to work. Do you understand me, Rit and Henry?" "Yes, Missus, we understand." And away we flew, laughing, and thinking it a great joke that we, Massa's pets, must learn to work.

But it was a sad, sad change on the old plantation, and the beautiful, proud Sunny South, with its masters and mistresses, was bowed beneath the sin brought about by slavery. It was a terrible blow to the owners of plantations and slaves, and their children would feel it more than they, for they had been reared to be waited upon by willing or unwilling slaves.

In this place I will insert a poem my young mistress taught us, for she was always reading poems and good stories. But first I will record a talk I heard between my master and mistress. They were sitting in the dining-room, and we children were standing around the table. My mistress said, "I suppose, as Nancy has never returned, we had better keep Henry, Caroline and Louise until they are of age." "Yes, we will," said Massa, Miss Mary and Miss Martha, "but it is 'man proposes and God disposes.'"

So in the following pages you will read the sequel to my childhood life in the Sunny South.

Right after the war when my mother had got settled in her hut, with her little brood hovered around her, from which she had been so long absent, we had nothing to eat, and nothing to sleep on save some old pieces of horse-blankets and hay that the soldiers gave her. The first day in the hut was a rainy day; and as night drew near it grew more fierce, and we children had gathered some little fagots to make a fire by the time mother came home, with something for us to eat, such as she had gathered through the day. It was only corn meal and pease and ham-bone and skins which she had for our supper. She had started a little fire, and said, "Some of you close that door," for it was cold. She swung the pot over the fire and filled it with the pease and ham-bone and skins. Then she seated her little brood around the fire on the pieces of blanket, where we watched with all our eyes, our hearts filled with desire, looking to see what she would do next. She took down an old broken earthen bowl, and tossed into it the little meal she had brought, stirring it up with water, making a hoe cake. She said, "One of you draw that griddle out here," and she placed it on the few little coals. Perhaps this griddle you have never seen, or one like it. I will describe it to you. This griddle was a round piece of iron, quite thick, having three legs. It might have been made in a blacksmith's shop, for I have never seen one like it before or since. It was placed upon the coals, and with an old iron spoon she put on this griddle half of the corn meal she had mixed up. She said, "I will put a tin plate over this, and put it away for your breakfast." We five children were eagerly watching the pot boiling, with the pease and ham-bone. The rain was pattering on the roof of the hut. All at once there came a knock at the door. My mother answered the knock. When she opened the door, there stood a white woman and three little children, all dripping with the rain. My mother said, "In the name of the Lord, where are you going on such a night, with these children?" The woman said, "Auntie, I am travelling. Will you please let me stop here to-night, out of the rain, with my children?" My mother said, "Yes, honey. I ain't got much, but what I have got I will share with you." "God bless you!" They all came in. We children looked in wonder at what had come. But my mother scattered her own little brood and made a place for the forlorn wanderers. She said, "Wait, honey, let me turn over that hoe cake." Then the two women fell to talking, each telling a tale of woe. After a time, my mother called out, "Here, you, Louise, or some one of you, put some fagots under the pot, so these pease can get done." We couldn't put them under fast enough, first one and then another of us children, the mothers still talking. Soon my mother said, "Draw that hoe cake one side, I guess it is done." My mother said to the woman, "Honey, ain't you got no husband?" She said, "No, my husband got killed in the war." My mother replied, "Well, my husband died right after the war. I have been away from my little brood for four years. With a hard struggle, I have got them away from the Farrin plantation, for they did not want to let them go. But I got them. I was determined to have them. But they would not let me have them if they could have kept them. With God's help I will keep them from starving. The white folks are good to me. They give me work, and I know, with God's help, I can get along." The white woman replied, "Yes, Auntie, my husband left me on a rich man's plantation. This man promised to look out for me until my husband came home; but he got killed in the war, and the Yankees have set his negroes free and he said he could not help me any more, and we would have to do the best we could for ourselves. I gave my things to a woman to keep for me until I could find my kinsfolk. They live about fifty miles from here, up in the country. I am on my way there now." My mother said, "How long will it take you to get there?" "About three days, if it don't rain." My mother said, "Ain't you got some way to ride there?" "No, Auntie, there is no way of riding up where my folks live, the place where I am from."

We hoped the talk was most ended, for we were anxiously watching that pot. Pretty soon my mother seemed to realize our existence. She exclaimed, "My Lord! I suppose the little children are nearly starved. Are those pease done, young ones?" She turned and said to the white woman, "Have you-all had anything to eat?" "We stopped at a house about dinner time, but the woman didn't have anything but some bread and buttermilk." My mother said, "Well, honey, I ain't got but a little, but I will divide with you." The woman said, "Thank you, Auntie. You just give my children a little; I can do without it."

Then came the dividing. We all watched with all our eyes to see what the shares would be. My mother broke a mouthful of bread and put it on each of the tin plates. Then she took the old spoon and equally divided the pea soup. We children were seated around the fire, with some little wooden spoons. But the wooden spoons didn't quite go round, and some of us had to eat with our fingers. Our share of the meal, however, was so small that we were as hungry when we finished as when we began.

My mother said, "Take that rag and wipe your face and hands, and give it to the others and let them use it, too. Put those plates upon the table." We immediately obeyed orders, and took our seats again around the fire. "One of you go and pull that straw out of the corner and get ready to go to bed." We all lay down on the straw, the white children with us, and my mother covered us over with the blanket. We were soon in the "Land of Nod," forgetting our empty stomachs. The two mothers still continued to talk, sitting down on the only seats, a couple of blocks. A little back against the wall my mother and the white woman slept.

Bright and early in the morning we were called up, and the rest of the hoe cake was eaten for breakfast, with a little meat, some coffee sweetened with molasses. The little wanderers and their mother shared our meal, and then they started again on their journey towards their home among their kinsfolk, and we never saw them again. My mother said, "God bless you! I wish you all good luck. I hope you will reach your home safely." Then mother said to us, "You young ones put away that straw and sweep up the place, because I have to go to my work." But she came at noon and brought us a nice dinner, more satisfactory than the supper and breakfast we had had. We children were delighted that there were no little white children to share our meal this time.

In time, my older sister, Caroline, and myself got work among good people, where we soon forgot all the hard times in the little log cabin by the roadside in Clayton, Alabama.

Up to my womanhood, even to this day, these memories fill my mind. Some kind friends' eyes may see these pages, and may they recall some fond memories of their happy childhood, as what I have written brings back my young life in the great Sunny South.

I am something of the type of Moses on this 49th birthday; not that I am wrapped in luxuries, but that my thoughts are wrapped in the luxuries of the heavenly life in store for me, when my life work is done, and my friends shall be blessed by the work I shall have done. For God has commanded me to write this book, that some one may read and receive comfort and courage to do what God commands them to do. God bless every soul who shall read this true life story of one born in slavery.

It is now six years since the inspiration to write this book came to me in the Franklin evening school. I have struggled on, helped by friends. God said, "Write the book and I will help you." And He has.

It was through a letter of my life that the principal of the Franklin school said, "Write the book and I will help you." But he died before the next term, and I worked on. On this, my 49th birthday, I can say I believe that the book is close to the finish.

> My life is like the summer rose
> That opens to the morning sky,
> But ere the shades of evening close

Is scattered on the ground to die.
Yet on the rose's humble bed

The sweetest dews of night are shed,
As if she wept a tear for me,
As if she wept the waste to see.

My life is like the autumn leaf
That trembles in the moon's pale ray.
Its hold is frail, its date is brief,
Restless, and soon to pass away.
Yet, ere that leaf shall fall and fade,
The parent tree will mourn its shade,
The winds bewail the leafless tree;
But none shall breathe a sigh for me.

My life is like the prints which feet
Have left on Tampa's desert strand.
Soon as the rising tide shall beat
All trace will vanish from the sand.
Yet, as if grieving to efface
All vestige of the human race,
On that lone shore loud moans the sea.
But none, alas, shall mourn for me.

A VISION

There remains to be told the story of my conversion and how I
came to write the foregoing history of my life.

In 1875 I was taken sick. I thought I was going to die, and I
promised the Lord I would serve Him if he would only spare my
life. When I got well again, however, I forgot all about my
promise. Then I was taken sick again. It seemed I had to go
through a dark desert place, where great demons stood on
either side. In the distance I could just see a dim light, and I
tried to get to this light, but could not reach it. Then I found
myself in a great marsh, and was sinking. I threw up my hands
and said, "Lord, if Thou wilt raise me from this pit, I will never

fail to serve Thee." Then it seemed as if I mounted on wings into the air, and all the demons that stood about made a great roaring. My flight ended on the top of a hill. But I was troubled because I could not find the light. All at once, at the sound of a loud peal of thunder, the earth opened, and I fell down into the pits of hell. Again I prayed to God to save me from this, and again I promised to serve Him. My prayer was answered, and I was able to fly out of the pit, on to a bank. At the foot of the little hill on which I sat were some little children, and they called to me to come down. But I could not get down. Then the children raised a ladder for me, and I came down among them. A little cherub took me by the hand and led me in the River of Badjied of Jordan. I looked at my ankles and shoulders and discovered I had little wings. On the river was a ship. The children, the cherub and I got into the ship. When we reached a beautiful spot, the little cherub made the ship fast, and there opened before us pearly gates, and we all passed through into the golden street. The street led to the throne of God, about which we marched. Then the cherub conducted us to a table where a feast was spread. Then the children vanished. The cherub took me by the hand, and said, "Go back into the world, and tell the saints and sinners what a Savior you have found, and if you prove faithful I will take you to Heaven to live forever, when I come again."

When I recovered from my sickness, I was baptized by the Rev. Dr. Pope, and joined the church in Macon. When I came North, I brought my letter. Not finding any church for colored people, I came among the white people, and was treated so kindly that I became very much attached to them. The first church I became connected with in the North, was in Newtonville. When I came to Boston, I went to the Warren Avenue Baptist Church. Before my marriage I joined Tremont Temple, when Dr. Lorimer was its pastor. When the church was burned, my letter was destroyed, but when I went South on a visit I had the letter duplicated, and took it to the new Temple. I am still a member of the Temple, and hope to remain there as long as God gives me life.

Five years ago, I began to go to the Franklin evening school.

Mr. Guild was the master. At one time he requested all the pupils to write the story of their lives, and he considered my composition so interesting he said he thought if I could work it up and enlarge upon it, I could write a book. He promised to help me. My teacher was Miss Emerson, and she was interested in me. But the next year Miss Emerson gave up teaching, and Mr. Guild died.

In each of the terms that I have attended, I have received the certificates showing that I have been regular and punctual in attendance, have maintained good deportment, and shown general proficiency in the studies. I would have graduated in 1907, had it not been for sickness.

Memoir of Old Elizabeth, A Coloured Woman

Memoir of Old Elizabeth,
A Coloured Woman

MEMOIR, &C.

In the following Narrative of "OLD ELIZABETH," which was taken mainly from her own lips in her 97th year, her simple language has been adhered to as strictly as was consistent with perspicuity and propriety.

I was born in Maryland in the year 1766. My parents were slaves. Both my father and mother were religious people, and belonged to the Methodist Society. It was my father's practice to read in the Bible aloud to his children every sabbath morning. At these seasons, when I was but five years old, I often felt the overshadowing of the Lord's Spirit, without at all understanding what it meant; and these incomes and influences continued to attend me until I was eleven years old, particularly when I was alone, by which I was preserved from doing anything that I thought was wrong.

In the eleventh year of my age, my master sent me to another farm, several miles from my parents, brothers, and sisters, which was a great trouble to me. At last I grew so lonely and sad I thought I should die, if I did not see my mother. I asked the overseer if I might go, but being positively denied, I concluded to go without his knowledge. When I reached home my mother was away. I set off and walked twenty miles before I found her. I staid with her for several days, and we returned together. Next day I was sent back to my new place, which renewed my sorrow.

31

At parting, my mother told me that I had "nobody in the wide world to look to but God." These words fell upon my heart with pondrous weight, and seemed to add to my grief. I went back repeating as I went, "none but God in the wide world." On reaching the farm, I found the overseer was displeased at me for going without his liberty. He tied me with a rope, and gave me some stripes of which I carried the marks for weeks.

After this time, finding as my mother said, I had none in the world to look to but God, I betook myself to prayer, and in every lonely place I found an altar. I mourned sore like a dove and chattered forth my sorrow, moaning in the corners of the field, and under the fences.

I continued in this state for about six months, feeling as though my head were waters, and I could do nothing but weep. I lost my appetite, and not being able to take enough food to sustain nature, I became so weak I had but little strength to work; still I was required to do all my duty. One evening, after the duties of the day were ended, I thought I could not live over the night, so threw myself on a bench, expecting to die, and without being prepared to meet my Maker; and my spirit cried within me, must I die in this state, and be banished from Thy presence forever? I own I am a sinner in Thy sight, and not fit to live where thou art. Still it was my fervent desire that the Lord would pardon me. Just at this season, I saw with my spiritual eye, an awful gulf of misery. As I thought I was about to plunge into it, I heard a voice saying, "rise up and pray," which strengthened me. I fell on my knees and prayed the best I could the Lord's prayer. Knowing no more to say, I halted, but continued on my knees. My spirit was then *taught* to pray, "Lord, have mercy on me—Christ save me." Immediately there appeared a director, clothed in white raiment. I thought he took me by the hand and said, "come with me." He led me down a long journey to a fiery gulf, and left me standing upon the brink of this awful pit. I began to scream for mercy, thinking I was about to be plunged to the belly of hell, and believed I should sink to endless ruin. Although I prayed and wrestled with all my might, it seemed in vain. Still, I felt all the while that I was sustained by some invisible power. At this solemn moment, I thought I saw a hand from which hung, as it were, a silver hair, and a voice told me that all the hope I had of being saved was no more than a hair; still, pray, and it will be sufficient. I then renewed my struggle, crying for mercy and salvation, until I found that every cry raised me higher and higher, and my head was quite above the fiery pillars. Then I thought I was permitted to look straight forward, and saw the Saviour standing with His hand stretched out to receive me. An indescribably glorious light was *in* Him, and He said, "peace, peace, come unto me." At this moment I felt that my sins were forgiven me, and the time of my deliverance was at hand. I sprang forward and fell at his feet, giving Him all the thanks and highest praises, crying, Thou hast redeemed me—Thou hast redeemed me to thyself. I felt filled with light and love. At this moment I thought my former guide took me again by the hand and led me upward, till I came to the celestial world and to heaven's door, which I saw was open, and while I stood there, a power surrounded me which drew me in, and I saw millions of glorified spirits in white robes. After I had this view, I thought I heard a voice saying, "Art thou willing to be saved?" I said, Yes Lord. Again I was asked, "Art thou willing to be saved in my way?" I stood speechless until he asked me again, "Art thou willing to be saved in my way?" Then I heard a whispering voice say, "If thou art not saved in the Lord's way, thou canst not be saved at all;" at which I exclaimed, "Yes Lord, in thy own way." Immediately a light fell upon my head, and I was filled with light, and I was shown the world lying in wickedness, and was told I must go there, and call the people to repentance, for the day of the Lord was at hand; and this message was as a heavy yoke upon me, so that I wept bitterly at the thought of what I should have to pass through. While I wept, I heard a voice say, "weep not, some will laugh at thee, some will scoff at thee, and the dogs will bark at thee, but while thou doest my will, I will be with thee to the ends of the earth."

I was at this time not yet thirteen years old. The next day, when I had come to myself, I felt like a new creature in Christ, and all my desire was to see the Saviour.

I lived in a place where there was no preaching, and no religious instruction; but every day I went out amongst the hay-stacks, where the presence of the Lord overshadowed me, and I was filled with sweetness and joy, and was as a vessel filled with holy oil. In this way I continued for about a year; many times while my hands were at my work, my spirit was carried away to spiritual things. One day as I was going to my old place behind the hay-stacks to pray, I was assailed with this language, "Are you going there to weep and pray? what a fool! there are older professors than you are, and they do not take that way to get to heaven; people whose sins are forgiven ought to be joyful and lively, and not be struggling and praying." With this I halted and concluded I would not go, but do as other professors did, and so went off to play; but at this moment the light that was in me became darkened, and the peace and joy that I once had, departed from me.

About this time I was moved back to the farm where my mother lived, and then sold to a stranger. Here I had deep sorrows and plungings, not having experienced a return of that sweet evidence and light with which I had been favoured formerly; but by watching unto prayer, and wrestling mightily with the Lord, my peace gradually returned, and with it a great exercise and weight upon my heart for the salvation of my fellow-creatures; and I was often carried to distant lands and shown places where I should have to travel and deliver the Lord's message. Years afterwards, I found myself visiting those towns and countries that I had seen in the light as I sat at home at my sewing,—places of which I had never heard.

Some years from this time I was sold to a Presbyterian for a term of years, as he did not think it right to hold slaves for life. Having served him faithfully my time out, he gave me my liberty, which was about the thirtieth year of my age.

As I now lived in a neighborhood where I could attend religious meetings, occasionally I felt moved to speak a few words therein; but I shrank from it—so great was the cross to my nature.

I did not speak much till I had reached my forty-second year, when it was revealed to me that the message which had been given to me I had not yet delivered, and the time had come. As I could read but little, I questioned within myself how it would be possible for me to deliver the message, when I did not understand the Scriptures. Whereupon I was moved to open a Bible that was near me, which I did, and my eyes fell upon this passage, "Gird up thy loins now like a man, and answer thou me. Obey God rather than man," &c. Here I fell into a great exercise of spirit, and was plunged very low. I went from one religious professor to another, enquiring of them what ailed me; but of all these I could find none who could throw any light upon such impressions. They all told me there was nothing in Scripture that would sanction such exercises. It was hard for men to travel, and what would women do? These things greatly discouraged me, and shut up my way, and caused me to resist the Spirit. After going to all that were accounted pious, and receiving no help, I returned to the Lord, feeling that I was nothing, and knew nothing, and wrestled and prayed to the Lord that he would fully reveal His will, and make the way plain.

Whilst I thus struggled, there seemed a light from heaven to fall upon me, which banished all my desponding fears, and I was enabled to form a new resolution to go on to prison and to death, if it might be my portion: and the Lord showed me that it was His will I should be resigned to die any death that might be my lot, in carrying his message, and be entirely crucified to the world, and sacrifice *all* to His glory that was then in my possession, which His witnesses, the holy Apostles, had done before me. It was then revealed to me that the Lord had given me the evidence of a clean heart, in which I could rejoice day and night, and I walked and talked with God, and my soul was illuminated with heavenly light, and I knew nothing but Jesus Christ, and him crucified.

One day, after these things, while I was at my work, the Spirit directed me to go to a poor widow, and ask her if I might have a meeting at her house, which was situated in one of the lowest and worst streets in Baltimore. With great joy she gave notice, and at the time appointed I appeared there among a few coloured sisters. When they had all prayed, they called upon me to close the meeting, and I felt an impression that I must say a few words; and while I was speaking, the house seemed filled with light; and when I was about to close the meeting, and was kneeling, a man came in and stood till I arose. It proved to be a watchman. The sisters became so frightened, they all went away except the one who lived in the house, and an old woman; they both appeared to be much frightened, fearing they should receive some personal injury, or be put out of the house. A feeling of weakness came over me for a short time, but I soon grew warm and courageous in the Spirit. The man then said to me, "I was sent here to break up your meeting. Complaint has been made to me that the people round here cannot sleep for the racket." I replied, "a good racket is better than a bad racket. How do they rest when the ungodly are dancing and fiddling till midnight? Why are not they molested by the watchmen? and why should we be for praising God, our Maker? Are we worthy of greater punishment for praying to Him? and are we to be prohibited from doing so, that sinners may remain slumbering in their sins?" While speaking these few words I grew warm with *heavenly* zeal, and laid my hand upon him and addressed him with gospel truth, "how do sinners sleep in hell, after slumbering in their sins here, and crying, 'let me rest, let me rest,' while sporting on the very brink of hell? Is the cause of God to be destroyed for this purpose?" Speaking several words more to this amount, he turned pale and trembled, and begged my pardon, acknowledging that it was not his wish to interrupt us, and that he would never disturb a religious assembly again. He then took leave of me in a comely manner and wished us success. After he was gone, I turned to the old sisters who by this time were quite cheered up. You see, said I, if the sisters had not fled, what a victory we might have had on the Lord's side; for the man seemed ready to give up under conviction. If it had not been for their cowardice, we might have all bowed in prayer, and a shout of victory had been heard amongst us.

Our meeting gave great offence, and we were forbid holding any more assemblies. Even the elders of our meeting joined with the wicked people, and said such meetings must be stopped, and that woman quieted. But I was not afraid of any of them, and continued to go, and burnt with a zeal not my own. The old sisters were zealous sometimes, and at other times would sink under the cross. Thus they grew cold, at which I was much grieved. I proposed to them to ask the elders to send a brother, which was concluded upon.

We went on for several years, and the Lord was with us with great power it proved, to the conversion of many souls, and we continued to grow stronger.

I felt at times that I must exercise in the ministry, but when I rose upon my feet I felt ashamed, and so I went under a cloud for some time, and endeavoured to keep silence; but I could not quench the Spirit. I was rejected by the elders and rulers, as Christ was rejected by the Jews before me, and while others were excused in crimes of the darkest dye, I was hunted down in every place where I appointed a meeting. Wading through many sorrows, I thought at times I might as well be banished from this life, as to feel the Almighty drawing me one way, and man another; so that I was tempted to cast myself into the dock. But contemplating the length of eternity, and how long my sufferings would be in that unchangeable world, compared with this, if I endured a little longer, the Lord was pleased to deliver me from this gloomy, melancholy state in his own time; though while this temptation lasted I roved up and down, and talked and prayed.

I often felt that I was unfit to assemble with the congregation with whom I had gathered, and had sometimes been made to rejoice in the Lord. I felt that I was despised on account of this gracious calling, and was looked upon as a speckled bird by the ministers to whom I looked for instruction, and to whom I resorted every opportunity for the same; but when I would converse with them, some would cry out, "You are an enthusiast"; and others said, "the Discipline did not allow of any such division of the work"; until I began to think I surely must be wrong. Under this reflection, I had another gloomy cloud to struggle through; but after awhile I felt much moved upon by the Spirit of the Lord, and meeting with an aged sister, I found upon conversing with her that she could sympathize with me in this spiritual work. She was the first one I had met with, who could fully understand my exercises. She offered to open her house for a meeting, and run the risk of all the church would do to her for it. Many were afraid to open their houses in this way, lest they should be turned out of the church.

I persevered, notwithstanding the opposition of those who were looked upon as higher and wiser. The meeting was appointed, and but few came. I felt much backwardness, and as though I could not pray, but a pressure upon me to arise and express myself by way of exhortation. After hesitating for some time whether I would take up the cross or no, I arose, and after expressing a few words, the Spirit came upon me with life, and a victory was gained over the power of darkness, and we could rejoice together in His love.

As for myself, I was so full I hardly knew whether I was in the body, or out of the body—so great was my joy for the victory on the Lord's side. But the persecution against me increased, and a complaint was carried forward, as was done formerly against Daniel, the servant of God, and the elders came out with indignation for my holding meetings contrary to discipline—being a woman.

Thus we see when the heart is not inspired, and the inward eye enlightened by the Spirit, we are incapable of discerning the mystery of God in these things. Individuals creep into the church that are unregenerate, and after they have been there awhile, they fancy that they have got the grace of God, while they are destitute of it. They may have a degree of light in their heads, but evil in their hearts; which makes them think they are qualified to be judges of the ministry, and their conceit makes them very busy in matters of religion, judging of the revelations that are given to others, while they have received none themselves. Being thus mistaken, they are calculated to make a great deal of confusion in the church, and clog the true ministry.

These are they who eat their own bread, and wear their own apparel, having the form of godliness, but are destitute of the power.

Again I felt encouraged to attend another and another appointment. At one of these meetings, some of the class-leaders were present, who were constrained to cry out, "Surely the Lord has *revealed* these things to her" and asked one another if they ever heard the like? I look upon man as a very selfish being, when placed in a religious office, to presume to resist the work of the Almighty; because He does not work by man's authority. I did not faint under discouragement, but pressed on.

Under the contemplation of these things, I slept but little, being much engaged in receiving the revelations of the Divine will concerning this work, and the mysterious call thereto.

I felt very unworthy and small, notwithstanding the Lord had shown himself with great power, insomuch that conjecturers and critics were constrained to join in praise to his great name; for truly, we had times of refreshing from the presence of the Lord. At one of the meetings, a vast number of the white inhabitants of the place, and many coloured people, attended—many no doubt from curiosity to hear what the old coloured woman had to say. One, a great scripturian, fixed himself behind the door with pen and ink, in order to take down the discourse in short-hand; but the Almighty Being anointed me with such a portion of his Spirit, that he cast away his paper and pen, and heard the discourse with patience, and was much affected, for the Lord wrought powerfully on his heart. After meeting, he came forward and offered me his hand with solemnity on his countenance, and handed me something to pay for my conveyance home.

I returned, much strengthened by the Lord's power, to go on to the fulfilment of His work, although I was again pressed by the authorities of the church to which I belonged, for imprudency; and so much condemned, that I was sorely tempted by the enemy to turn aside into the wilderness. I was so embarrassed and encompassed, I wondered within myself whether all that were called to be mouth piece for the Lord, suffered such deep wadings as I experienced.

I now found I had to travel still more extensively in the work of the ministry, and I applied to the Lord for direction. I was often *invited* to go hither and thither, but felt that I must wait for the dictates of His Spirit.

At a meeting which I held in Maryland, I was led to speak from the passage, "Woe to the rebellious city," &c. After the meeting, the people came where I was, to take me before the squire; but the Lord delivered me from their hands.

I also held meetings in Virginia. The people there would not believe that a coloured woman could preach. And moreover, as she had no learning, they strove to imprison me because I spoke against slavery: and being brought up, they asked by what authority I spake? and if I had been ordained? I answered, not by the commission of men's hands: if the Lord had ordained me, I needed nothing better.

As I travelled along through the land, I was led at different times to converse with white men who were by profession ministers of the gospel. Many of them, up and down, confessed they did not believe in revelation, which gave me to see that men were sent forth as ministers without Christ's authority. In a conversation with one of these, he said, "You think you have these things by revelation, but there has been no such thing as revelation since Christ's ascension." I asked him where the apostle John got his revelation while he was in the Isle of Patmos. With this, he rose up and left me, and I said in my spirit, get thee behind me Satan.

I visited many remote places, where there were no meeting houses, and held many glorious meetings, for the Lord poured out his Spirit in sweet effusions. I also travelled in Canada, and visited several settlements of coloured people, and felt an open door amongst them.

I may here remark, that while journeying through the different states of the Union, I met with many of the Quaker Friends, and visited them in their families. I received much kindness and sympathy, and no opposition from them, in the prosecution of my labours.

On one occasion, in a thinly settled part of the country, seeing a Friend's meeting house open, I went in; at the same time a Friend and his little daughter followed me. We three composed the meeting. As we sat there in silence, I felt a remarkable overshadowing of the Divine presence, as much so as I ever experienced any where. Toward the close, a few words seemed to be given me, which I expressed, and left the place greatly refreshed in Spirit. From thence I went to Michigan, where I found a wide field of labour amongst my own colour. Here I remained four years. I established a school for coloured orphans, having always felt the great importance of the religious and moral *agri*culture of children, and the great need of it, especially amongst the coloured people. Having white teachers, I met with much encouragement.

My eighty-seventh year had now arrived, when suffering from disease, and feeling released from travelling further in my good Master's cause, I came on to Philadelphia, where I have remained until this time, which brings me to my ninety-seventh year. When I went forth, it was without purse or scrip,—and I have come through great tribulation and temptation—not by any might of my own, for I feel that I am but as dust and ashes before my almighty Helper, who has, according to His promise, been with me and sustained me through all, and gives me now firm faith that he will be with me to the end, and, in his own good time, receive me into His everlasting rest.

The Story of Mattie J. Jackson

The Story of Mattie J. Jackson
Written and arranged by
Dr. L. S. Thompson

PREFACE

The object in publishing this book is to gain sympathy from the earnest friends of those who have been bound down by a dominant race in circumstances over which they had no control—a butt of ridicule and a mark of oppression; over whom weary ages of degradation have passed. As the links have been broken and the shackles fallen from them through the unwearied efforts of our beloved martyr President Lincoln, as one I feel it a duty to improve the mind, and have ever had a thirst for education to fill that vacuum for which the soul has ever yearned since my earliest remembrance.

Thus I ask you to buy my little book to aid me in obtaining an education, that I may be enabled to do some good in behalf of the elevation of my emancipated brothers and sisters. I have now arrived at the age of twenty. As the first dawn of morning has passed, and the meridian of life is approaching, I know of no other way to speedily gain my object than through the aid and patronage of the friends of humanity.

NOTE Miss Jackson sustains a high moral character—has been much respected since she has been in Lawrence. She is from St. Louis, Missouri, and arrived here on the 11th of April, 1866. To gain the wish of the heart is utterly impossible without

44

more means than she can obtain otherwise. Her friends have borne her expenses to Lawrence, and have and are still willing to render her aid as far their limited means will allow. She was in the same condition of all the neglected and oppressed. Her personal requirements are amply supplied. She now only craves the means to clothe and qualify the intellect. My humble prayer is that she may meet with unlimited success.

This young lady is highly worthy of all the aid our kind friends feel a duty to bestow upon her. She purposes lecturing and relating her story; and I trust she may render due satisfaction and bear some humble part in removing doubts indulged by the prejudices against the natural genius and talent of our race. May God give her grace and speed her on her way.

Respectfully yours,
L. S. T.

MATTIE'S STORY

My ancestors were transported from Africa to America at the time the slave trade flourished in the Eastern States. I cannot give dates, as my progenitors, being slaves, had no means of keeping them. By all accounts my great grandfather was captured and brought from Africa. His original name I never learned. His master's name was Jackson, and he resided in the State of New York. My grandfather was born in the same State, and also remained a slave for some length of time, when he was emancipated, his master presenting him with quite an amount of property. He was true, honest and responsible, and this present was given him as a reward. He was much encouraged by the cheering prospect of better days. A better condition of things now presented itself. As he possessed a large share of confidence, he came to the conclusion, as he was free, that he was capable of selecting his own residence and manage his own affairs with prudence and economy. But, alas, his hopes were soon blighted. More heart rending sorrow and degradation awaited him. He was earnestly invited by a white decoyer to relinquish his former design and accompany him to Missouri and join him in speculation and become wealthy. As partners, they embarked on board a schooner for St. Charles, Mo. On the passage, my grandfather was seized with a fever, and for a while was totally unconscious. When he regained his reason he found himself, near his journey's end, divested of his free papers and all others. On his arrival at St. Charles he was seized by a huge, surly looking slaveholder who claimed him as his property. The contract had previously been concluded by his Judas-like friend, who had received the bounty. Oh, what a sad disappointment.

After serving for thirty years to be thrust again into bondage where a deeper degredation and sorrow and hopeless toil were to be his portion for the remaining years of his existence. In deep despair and overwhelmed with grief, he made his escape to the woods, determined to put an end to his sorrows by perishing with cold and hunger. His master immediately pursued him, and in twenty-four hours found him with hands and feet frost-bitten, in consequence of which he lost the use of his fingers and toes, and was thenceforth of little use to his new master. He remained with him, however, and married a woman in the same station in life. They lived as happily as their circumstances would permit. As Providence allotted, they only had one son, which was my father, Westly Jackson. He had a deep affection for his family, which the slave ever cherishes for his dear ones. He had no other link to fasten him to the human family but his fervent love for those who were bound to him by love and sympathy in their wrongs and sufferings. My grandfather remained in the same family until his death. My father, Westly Jackson, married, at the age of twenty-two, a girl owned by James Harris, named Ellen Turner. Nothing of importance occurred until three years after their marriage, when her master, Harris failed through the extravagance and mismanagement of his wife, who was a great spendthrift and a dreaded terror to the poor slaves and all others with whom she associated in common circumstances, consequently the entire stock was sold by the sheriff to a trader residing in Virginia. On account of the good reputation my mother sustained as a worthy servant and excellent cook, a tyrannical and much dreaded slave-holder watched for an opportunity to purchase her, but fortunately arrived a few moments too late, and she was bid off in too poor a condition of health to remain long a subject of banter and speculation. Her husband was allowed to carefully lift her down from the block and accompany her to her new master's, Charles Canory, who treated her very kindly while she remained in his family. Mr. Canory resided in St. Charles County for five years after he purchased my mother. During that time my father and mother were in the same neighborhood, but a short distance from each other. But another trial awaited them. Her master removed twenty miles away to a village called Bremen, near

St. Louis, Mo. My father, thereafter, visited my mother once a week, walking the distance every Saturday evening and returning on Sunday evening. But through all her trials and deprivations her trust and confidence was in Him who rescued his faithful followers from the fiery furnace and the lion's den, and led Moses through the Red Sea. Her trust and confidence was in Jesus. She relied on His precious promises, and ever found Him a present help in every time of need. Two years after this separation my father was sold and separated from us, but previous to his delivery to his new master he made his escape to a free State. My mother was then left with two children. She had three during the time they were permitted to remain together, and buried one. Their names were Sarah Ann, Mattie Jane and Esther J. When my father left I was about three years of age, yet I can well remember the little kindnesses my father used to bestow upon us, and the deep affection and fondness he manifested for us. I shall never forget the bitter anguish of my parents' hearts, the sighs they uttered or the profusion of tears which coursed down their sable checks. O, what a horrid scene, but he was not her's, for cruel hands had separated them.

> The strongest tie of earthly joy that bound the aching
>   heart—
> His love was e'er a joyous light that o'er the pathway
>   shone—
> A fountain gushing ever new amid life's desert wild—
> His slightest word was a sweet tone of music round her
>   heart—
> Their lives a streamlet blent in one. O, Father, must
>   they part?
> They tore him from her circling arms, her last and fond
>   embrace—
> O never again can her sad eyes gaze upon his mournful
>   face.
> It is not strange these bitter sighs are constant bursting
>   forth.
> Amid mirth and glee and revelry she never took a part,
> She was a mother left alone with sorrow in her heart.

But my mother was conscious some time previous of the change that was to take place with my father, and if he was sold in the immediate vicinity he would be likely to be sold again at their will, and she concluded to assist him to make his escape from bondage. Though the parting was painful, it afforded her solace in the contemplation of her husband becoming a free man, and cherishing a hope that her little family, through the aid of some angel of mercy, might be enabled to make their escape also, and meet to part no more on earth. My father came to spend the night with us, according to his usual custom. It was the last time, and sadness brooded upon his brow. It was the only opportunity he had to make his escape without suspicion and detection, as he was immediately to fall into the hands of a new master. He had never been sold from the place of his birth before, and was determined never to be sold again if God would verify his promise. My father was not educated, but was a preacher, and administered the Word of God according to the dictation and revelation of the spirit. His former master had allowed him the privilege of holding meetings in the village within the limits of his pass on the Sundays when he visited my mother. But on this Saturday evening he arrived and gave us all his farewell kiss, and hurried away. My mother's people were aware of my father's intention, but rather than spare my mother, and for fear she might be detected, they secreted his escape. His master called a number of times and enquired for him and strongly pressed my mother to give him an account of my father, but she never gave it. We waited patiently, hoping to learn if he succeeded in gaining his freedom. Many anxious weeks and months passed before we could get any tidings from him, until at length my mother heard that he was in Chicago, a free man and preaching the Gospel. He made every effort to get his family, but all in vain. The spirit of slavery so strongly existed that letters could not reach her; they were all destroyed. My parents had never learned the rescuing scheme of the underground railroad which had borne so many thousands to the standard of freedom and victories. They knew no other resource than to depend upon their own chance in running away and secreting themselves. If caught they were in a worse condition than before.

THEIR ATTEMPT
TO MAKE THEIR ESCAPE

Two years after my father's departure, my mother, with her two
children, my sister and myself, attempted to make her escape.
After traveling two days we reached Illinois. We slept in the
woods at night. I believe my mother had food to supply us but
fasted herself. But the advertisement had reached there before
us, and loafers were already in search of us, and as soon as we
were discovered on the brink of the river one of the spies made
enquiries respecting her suspicious appearance. She was aware
that she was arrested, consequently she gave a true account of
herself—that she was in search of her husband. We were then
destitute of any articles of clothing excepting our wearing
apparel. Mother had become so weary that she was compelled
to leave our package of clothing on the way. We were taken back
to St. Louis and committed to prison and remained there one
week, after which they put us in Linch's trader's yard, where we
remained about four weeks. We were then sold to William
Lewis. Mr. Lewis was a very severe master, and inflicted such
punishment upon us as he thought proper. However, I only
remember one severe contest Mr. Lewis had with my mother.
For some slight offence Mrs. Lewis became offended and was
tartly and loudly reprimanding her, when Mr. L. came in and
rashly felled her to the floor with his fist. But his wife was constantly pulling our ears, snapping us with her thimble, rapping
us on the head and the sides of it. It appeared impossible to
please her. When we first went to Mr. L.'s they had a cowhide
which she used to inflict on a little slave girl she previously
owned, nearly every night. This was done to learn the little girl
to wake early to wait on her children. But my mother was a
cook, as I before stated, and was in the habit of roasting meats
and toasting bread. As they stinted us for food my mother
roasted the cowhide. It was rather poor picking, but it was the
last cowhide my mother ever had an opportunity to cook while
we remained in his family. Mr. L. soon moved about six miles

from the city and entered in partnership with his brother-in-law. The servants were then divided and distributed in both families. It unfortunately fell to my lot to live with Mrs. Larry, my mistress' sister, which rendered my condition worse than the first. My master even disapproved of my ill treatment and took me to another place; the place my mother resided before my father's escape. After a short time Mr. Lewis again returned to the city. My mother still remained as cook in his family. After six years' absence of my father my mother married again a man by the name of George Brown, and lived with her second husband about four years, and had two children, when he was sold for requesting a different kind and enough food. His master considered it a great insult, and declared he would sell him. But previous to this insult, as he called it, my step-father was foreman in Mr. L.'s tobacco factory. He was trusty and of good moral habits, and was calculated to bring the highest price in the human market; therefore the excuse to sell him for the above offence was only a plot. The morning this offence occurred, Mr. L. bid my father to remain in the kitchen till he had taken his breakfast. After pulling his ears and slapping his face bade him come to the factory; but instead of going to the factory he went to Canada. Thus my poor mother was again left alone with two more children added to her misery and sorrow to toil on her weary pilgrimage.

> Racked with agony and pain she was left alone again,
> With a purpose nought could move
> And the zeal of woman's love,
> Down she knelt in agony
> To ask the Lord to clear the way.

> True she said O gracious Lord,
> True and faithful is thy word;
> But the humblest, poorest, may
> Eat the crumbs they cast away.

> Though nine long years had passed
> Without one glimmering light of day

She never did forget to pray
And has not yet though whips and chains are cast away.

For thus said the blessed Lord,
I will verify my word;
By the faith that has not failed,
Thou hast asked and shall prevail.

We remained but a short time at the same residence when Mr. Lewis moved again to the country. Soon after, my little brother was taken sick in consequence of being confined in a box in which my mother was obliged to keep him. If permitted to creep around the floor her mistress thought it would take too much time to attend to him. He was two years old and never walked. His limbs were perfectly paralyzed for want of exercise. We now saw him gradually failing, but was not allowed to render him due attention. Even the morning he died she was compelled to attend to her usual work. She watched over him for three months by night and attended to her domestic affairs by day. The night previous to his death we were aware he could not survive through the approaching day, but it made no impression on my mistress until she came into the kitchen and saw his life fast ebbing away, then she put on a sad countenance for fear of being exposed, and told my mother to take the child to her room, where he only lived one hour. When she found he was dead she ordered grave clothes to be brought and gave my mother time to bury him. O that morning, that solemn morning. It appears to me that when that little spirit departed as though all heaven rejoiced and angels veiled their faces.

My mother too in concert joined,—
Her mingled praise with them combined.
Her little saint had gone to God
Who saved him with his precious blood.

Who said "Suffer little children to come unto me and forbid them not."

THE SOLDIERS, AND OUR TREATMENT
DURING THE WAR

Soon after the war commenced the rebel soldiers encamped near Mr. Lewis' residence, and remained there one week. They were then ordered by General Lyons to surrender, but they refused. There were seven thousand Union and seven hundred rebel soldiers. The Union soldiers surrounded the camp and took them and exhibited them through the city and then confined them in prison. I told my mistress that the Union soldiers were coming to take the camp. She replied that it was false, that it was General Kelly coming to re-enforce Gen. Frost. In a few moments the alarm was heard. I told Mrs. L. the Unionists had fired upon the rebels. She replied it was only the salute of Gen. Kelly. At night her husband came home with the news that Camp Jackson was taken and all the soldiers prisoners. Mrs. Lewis asked how the Union soldiers could take seven hundred men when they only numbered the same. Mr. L. replied they had seven thousand. She was much astonished, and cast her eye around to us for fear we might hear her. Her suspicion was correct; there was not a word passed that escaped our listening ears. My mother and myself could read enough to make out the news in the papers. The Union soldiers took much delight in tossing a paper over the fence to us. It aggravated my mistress very much. My mother used to sit up nights and read to keep posted about the war. In a few days my mistress came down to the kitchen again with another bitter complaint that it was a sad affair that the Unionists had taken their delicate citizens who had enlisted and made prisoners of them—that they were babes. My mother reminded her of taking Fort Sumpter and Major Anderson and serving them the same and that turn about was fair play. She then hastened to her room with the speed of a deer, nearly unhinging every door in her flight, replying as she went that the Niggers and Yankees were seeking to take the country. One day, after she had visited the kitchen to superintend some domestic affairs, as she pretended, she became very angry without a word being passed, and said—"I think it has come to a pretty pass, that old Lincoln, with his long legs, an old rail splitter, wishes to put the Niggers on an equality with the whites; that her children should never be on an equal footing with a Nigger. She had rather see them dead." As my mother made no reply to her remarks, she stopped talking, and commenced venting her spite on my companion servant. On one occasion Mr. Lewis searched my mother's room and found a picture of President Lincoln, cut from a newspaper, hanging in her room. He asked her what she was doing with old Lincoln's picture. She replied it was there because she liked it. He then knocked her down three times, and sent her to the trader's yard for a month as punishment. My mistress indulged some hopes till the victory of New Orleans, when she heard the famous Union song sang to the tune of Yankee Doodle:

> The rebels swore that New Orleans never should be taken,
> But if the Yankees came so near they should not save their bacon
> That's the way they blustered when they thought they were so handy,
> But Farragut steamed up one day and gave them Doodle Dandy.

> Ben. Butler then was ordered down to regulate the city;
> He made the rebels walk a chalk, and was not that a pity?
> That's the way to serve them out—that's the way to treat them,
> They must not go and put on airs after we have beat them.

> He made the rebel banks shell out and pay the loyal people,
> He made them keep the city clean from pig's sty to church steeple.
> That's the way Columbia speaks, let all men believe her;
> That's the way Columbia speaks instead of yellow fever.
> He sent the saucy women up and made them treat us well

He helped the poor and snubbed the rich; they thought
   he was the devil,
Bully for Ben. Butler, then, they thought he was so
   handy;
Bully for Ben Butler then,—Yankee Doodle Dandy.

The days of sadness for mistress were days of joy for us. We
shouted and laughed to the top of our voices. My mistress was
more enraged than ever—nothing pleased her. One evening,
after I had attended to my usual duties, and I supposed all was
complete, she, in a terrible rage, declared I should be punished
that night. I did not know the cause, neither did she. She went
immediately and selected a switch. She placed it in the corner
of the room to await the return of her husband at night for him
to whip me. As I was not pleased with the idea of a whipping I
bent the switch in the shape of W, which was the first letter of
his name, and after I had attended to the dining room my fellow
servant and myself walked away and stopped with an aunt of
mine during the night. In the morning we made our way to the
Arsenal, but could gain no admission. While we were wandering
about seeking protection, the girl's father overtook us and persuaded us to return home. We finally complied. All was quiet.
Not a word was spoken respecting our sudden departure. All
went on as usual. I was permitted to attend to my work without
interruption until three weeks after. One morning I entered
Mrs. Lewis' room, and she was in a room adjoining, complaining of something I had neglected. Mr. L. then enquired if I had
done my work. I told him I had. She then flew into a rage and
told him I was saucy, and to strike me, and he immediately gave
me a severe blow with a stick of wood, which inflicted a deep
wound upon my head. The blood ran over my clothing, which
gave me a frightful appearance. Mr. Lewis then ordered me to
change my clothing immediately. As I did not obey he became
more enraged, and pulled me into another room and threw me
on the floor, placed his knee on my stomach, slapped me on the
face and beat me with his fist, and would have punished me
more had not my mother interfered. He then told her to go

away or he would compel her to, but she remained until he left me. I struggled mightily, and stood him a good test for a while, but he was fast conquering me when my mother came. He was aware my mother could usually defend herself against one man, and both of us would overpower him, so after giving his wife strict orders to take me up stairs and keep me there, he took his carriage and drove away. But she forgot it, as usual. She was highly gratified with my appropriate treatment, as she called it, and retired to her room, leaving me to myself. I then went to my mother and told her I was going away. She bid me go, and added "May the Lord help you." I started for the Arsenal again and succeeded in gaining admittance and seeing the Adjutant. He ordered me to go to another tent, where there was a woman in similar circumstances, cooking. When the General found I was there he sent me to the boarding house. I remained there three weeks, and when I went I wore the same stained clothing as when I was so severely punished, which has left a mark on my head which will ever remind me of my treatment while in slavery. Thanks be to God, though tortured by wrong and goaded by oppression, the hearts that would madden with misery have broken the iron yoke.

MR. LEWIS CALLS AT
THE BOARDING HOUSE

At the expiration of three weeks Mr. Lewis called at my boarding house, accompanied by his brother-in-law, and enquired for me, and the General informed him where I was. He then told me my mother was very anxious for me to come home, and I returned. The General had ordered Mr. Lewis to call at headquarters, when he told him if he had treated me right I would not have been compelled to seek protection of him; that my first appearance was sufficient proof of his cruelty. Mr. L. promised to take me home and treat me kindly. Instead of fulfilling his promise he carried me to the trader's yard, where, to my great surprise, I found my mother. She had been there during my absence, where she was kept for fear she would find me and take my brother and sister and make her escape. There was so much excitement at that time, (1861), by the Union soldiers rendering the fugitives shelter and protection, he was aware that if she applied to them, as he did not fulfill his promise in my case, he would stand a poor chance. If my mother made application to them for protection they would learn that he did not return me home, and immediately detect the intrigue. After I was safely secured in the trader's yard, Mr. L. took my mother home. I remained in the yard three months. Near the termination of the time of my confinement I was passing by the office when the cook of the Arsenal saw and recognized me and informed the General that Mr. L. had disobeyed his orders, and had put me in the trader's yard instead of taking me home. The General immediately arrested Mr. L. and gave him one hundred lashes with the cow-hide, so that they might identify him by a scarred back, as well as his slaves. My mother had the pleasure of washing his stained clothes, otherwise it would not have been known. My master was compelled to pay three thousand dollars and let me out. He then put me to service, where I remained seven months, after which he came in great haste and took me into the city and put me into the trader's yard again. After he received the punishment he treated my mother and the children worse than ever, which caused her to take her children and secrete themselves in the city, and would have remained undetected had it not been for a traitor who pledged himself to keep the secret. But King Whiskey fired up his brain one evening, and out popped the secret. My mother and sister were consequently taken and committed to the trader's yard. My little brother was then eight years of age, my sister sixteen, and myself eighteen. We remained there two weeks, when a rough looking man, called Capt. Tirrell, came to the yard and enquired for our family. After he had examined us he remarked that we were a fine looking family, and bid us retire. In about two hours he returned, at the edge of the evening, with a covered wagon, and took my mother and brother and sister and left me. My mother refused to go without me, and told him she would raise an alarm. He advised her to remain as quiet as possible. At length she was compelled to go. When she entered the wagon there was a man standing behind with his hands on each side of the wagon to prevent her from making her escape. She sprang to her feet and gave this man a desperate blow, and leaping to the ground she made an alarm. The watchmen came to her assistance immediately, and there was quite a number of Union policemen guarding the city at that time, who rendered her due justice as far as possible. This was before the emancipation proclamation was issued. After she leaped from the wagon they drove on, taking her children to the boat. The police questioned my mother. She told them that Capt. Tirrell had put her children on board the boat, and was going to take them to Memphis and sell them into hard slavery. They accompanied her to the boat, and arrived just as they were casting off. The police ordered them to stop and immediately deliver up the children, who had been secreted in the Captain's private apartment. They were brought forth and returned. Slave speculation was forbidden in St. Louis at that time. The Union soldiers had possession of the city, but their power was limited to the suppression of the selling of slaves to go out of the city. Considerable smuggling was done, however, by pretending Unionism, which was the case with our family.

RELEASED FROM THE TRADER'S YARD
AND TAKEN TO HER NEW MASTER

Immediately after dinner my mother called for me to accompany her to our new home, the residence of the Captain, together with my brother and sister. We fared very well while we were there. Mrs. Tirrell was insane, and my mother had charge of the house. We remained there four months. The Captain came home only once a week and he never troubled us for fear we might desert him. His intention was to smuggle us away before the State became free. That was the understanding when he bought us of Mr. Lewis, as it was not much of an object to purchase slaves while the proclamation was pending, and they likely to lose all their property; but they would, for a trifle purchase a whole family of four or five persons to send out of the

State. Kentucky paid as much, or more than ever, for slaves. As they pretended to take no part in the rebellion they supposed they would be allowed to keep them without interference. Consequently the Captain's intention was to keep as quiet as possible till the excitement concerning us was over, and he could get us off without detection. Mr. Lewis would rather have disposed of us for nothing than have seen us free. He hated my mother in consequence of her desire for freedom, and her endeavors to teach her children the right way as far as her ability would allow. He also held a charge against her for reading the papers and understanding political affairs. When he found he was to lose his slaves he could not bear the idea of her being free. He thought it too hard, as she had raised so many tempests for him, to see her free and under her own control. He had tantalized her in every possible way to humiliate and annoy her; yet while he could demand her services he appreciated and placed perfect confidence in mother and family. None but a fiendish slaveholder could have rended an honest Christian heart in such a manner as this.

> Though it was her sad and weary lot to toil in slavery
> But one thing cheered her weary soul
> When almost in despair
> That she could gain a sure relief in attitude of prayer

CAPT. TIRRELL REMOVES THE
FAMILY—ANOTHER STRATEGY

One day the Captain commenced complaining of the expense of so large a family, and proposed to my mother that we should work out and he take part of the pay. My mother told him she would need what she earned for my little brother's support. Finally the Captain consented, and I was the first to be disposed of. The Captain took me in his buggy and carried me to the Depot, and I was put into a Union family, where I remained five months. Previous to my leaving, however, my mother and the Captain entered into a contract—he agreeing not to sell us, and

mother agreeing not to make her escape. While she was carrying out her promise in good faith, he was plotting to separate us.
We were all divided except mother and my little brother, who
remained together. My sister remained with one of the rebels,
but was tolerably treated. We all fared very well; but it was only
the calm before the rending tornado. Captain T. was Captain of
the boat to Memphis, from which the Union soldiers had rescued us. He commenced as a deck hand on the boat, then
attained a higher position, and continued to advance until he
became her Captain. At length he came in possession of slaves.
Then his accomplishments were complete. He was a very severe
slave master. Those mushroom slaveholders are much dreaded,
as their severity knows no bounds.

> Bondage and torture, scourges and chains
> Placed on our backs indelible stains.

I stated previously, in relating a sketch of my mother's history,
that she was married twice, and both husbands were to be sold
and made their escape. They both gained their freedom. One
was living,—the other died before the war. Both made every
effort to find us, but to no purpose. It was some years before we
got a correct account of her second husband, and he had no
account of her, except once he heard that mother and children
had perished in the woods while endeavoring to make their
escape. In a few years after his arrival in the free States he married again.

When about sixteen years of age, while residing with her original master, my mother became acquainted with a young man,
Mr. Adams, residing in a neighboring family, whom she much
respected; but he was soon sold, and she lost trace of him
entirely, as was the common occurrence with friends and companions though united by the nearest ties. When my mother
arrived at Captain Tirrell's, after leaving the boat, in her excitement she scarce observed anything except her little group so
miraculously saved from perhaps a final separation in this world.
She at length observed that the servant who was waiting to take
her to the Captain's residence in the country was the same man
with whom she formed the acquaintance when sixteen years old,

and they again renewed their acquaintance. He had been married and buried his wife. It appeared that his wife had been in Captain Tirrell's family many years, and he also, for some time. They had a number of children, and Capt. Tirrell had sold them down South. This cruel blow, assisted by severe flogging and other ill treatment, rendered the mother insane, and finally caused her death.

In agony close to her bosom she pressed,
The life of her heart, the child of her breast—
Oh love from its tenderness gathering might
Had strengthed her soul for declining age.

But she is free. Yes, she has gone from the land of the slave;
The hand of oppression must rest in the grave.
The blood hounds have missed the scent of her way,
The hunter is rifled and foiled of his prey.

After my mother had left the Captain to take care of herself and child, according to agreement with the Captain, she became engaged to Mr. Adams. He had bought himself previously for a large price. After they became acquainted, the Captain had an excellent opportunity of carrying out his stratagem. He commenced bestowing charity upon Mr. Adams. As he had purchased himself, and Capt. T. had agreed not to sell my mother, they had decided to marry at an early day. They hired a house in the city and were to commence housekeeping immediately. The Captain made him a number of presents and seemed much pleased with the arrangement. The day previous to the one set for the marriage, while they were setting their house in order, a man called and enquired for a nurse, pretending he wanted one of us. Mother was absent; he said he would call again, but he never came. On Wednesday evening we attended a protracted meeting. After we had returned home and retired, a loud rap was heard at the door. My Aunt enquired who was there. The reply was, "Open the door or I will break it down." In a moment in rushed seven men, four watchmen and three traders, and ordered mother to take my brother and me and follow them, which she hastened to do as fast as possible, but we were not

allowed time to put on our usual attire. They thrust us into a
close carriage. For fear of my mother alarming the citizens they
threw her to the ground and choked her until she was nearly
strangled, then pushed her into a coach. The night was dark and
dreary; the stars refused to shine, the moon to shed her light.

> 'Tis not strange the heavenly orbs
> In silence blushed 'neath Nature's sable garb
> When woman's gagged and rashly torn away
> Without blemish and without crime.
> Unheeded by God's holy word:—
> Unloose the fetters, break the chain,
> And make my people free again,
> And let them breath pure freedom's air
> And her rich bounty freely share.
> Let Eutopia stretch her bleeding hands abroad;
> Her cry of anguish finds redress from God.

We were hurried along the streets. The inhabitants heard our
cries and rushed to their doors, but our carriage being perfectly
tight, and the alarm so sudden, that we were at the jail before
they could give us any relief. There were strong Union men and
officers in the city, and if they could have been informed of the
human smuggling they would have released us. But oh, that horrid, dilapidated prison, with its dim lights and dingy walls, again
presented itself to our view. My sister was there first, and we
were thrust in and remained there until three o'clock the following afternoon. Could we have notified the police we should
have been released, but no opportunity was given us. It appears
that this kidnapping had been in contemplation from the time
we were before taken and returned; and Captain Tirrell's kindness to mother,—his benevolence towards Mr. Adams in assist-
ing him to furnish his house,—his generosity in letting us work
for ourselves,—his approbation in regard to the contemplated
marriage was only a trap. Thus instead of a wedding Thursday
evening, we were hurled across the ferry to Albany Court House
and to Kentucky through the rain and without our outer garments. My mother had lost her bonnet and shawl in the struggle while being thrust in the coach, consequently she had no

protection from the storm, and the rest of us were in similar circumstances. I believe we passed through Springfield. I think it
was the first stopping place after we left East St. Louis, and we
were put on board the cars and secreted in the gentlemen's
smoking car, in which there were only a few rebels. We arrived
in Springfield about twelve o'clock at night. When we took the
cars it was dark, bleak and cold. It was the 18th of March, and
as we were without bonnets and clothing to shield us from the
sleet and wind, we suffered intensely. The old trader, for fear
that mother might make her escape, carried my brother, nine
years of age, from one train to the other. We then took the cars
for Albany, and arrived at eight o'clock in the morning. We were
then carried on the ferry in a wagon. There was another family
in the wagon, in the same condition. We landed at Portland,
from thence to Louisville, and were put into John Clark's trader's
yard, and sold out separately, except my mother and little brother,
who were sold together. Mother remained in the trader's yard
two weeks, my sister six, myself four.

THE FARE AT THEIR NEW HOMES

Mother was sold to Captain Plasio. My sister to Benj. Board,
and myself to Capt. Ephraim Frisbee. The man who bought my
mother was a Spaniard. After she had been there a short time he
tried to have my mother let my brother stop at his saloon, a very
dissipated place, to wait upon his miserable crew, but my
mother objected. In spite of her objections he took him down to
try him, but some Union soldiers called at the saloon, and notic-
ing that he was very small, they questioned him, and my brother,
child like, divulged the whole matter. The Captain, fearful of
being betrayed and losing his property, let him continue with my
mother. The Captain paid eight hundred dollars for my mother
and brother. We were all sold for extravagant prices. My sister,
aged sixteen, was sold for eight hundred and fifty dollars; I was
sold for nine hundred dollars. This was in 1863. My mother was
cook and fared very well. My sister was sold to a single gentleman, whose intended took charge of her until they were mar-

ried, after which they took her to her home. She was her waiter, and fared as well as could be expected. I fared worse than either of the family. I was not allowed enough to eat, exposed to the cold, and not allowed through the cold winter to thoroughly warm myself once a month. The house was very large, and I could gain no access to the fire. I was kept constantly at work of the heaviest kind,—compelled to move heavy trunks and boxes,—many times to wash till ten and twelve o'clock at night. There were three deaths in the family while I remained there, and the entire burden was put upon me. I often felt to exclaim as the Children of Israel did: "O Lord, my burden is greater than I can bear." I was then seventeen years of age. My health has been impaired from that time to the present. I have a severe pain in my side by the slightest over exertion. In the Winter I suffer intensely with cold, and cannot get warm unless in a room heated to eighty degrees. I am infirm and burdened with the influence of slavery, whose impress will ever remain on my mind and body. For six months I tried to make my escape. I used to rise at four o'clock in the morning to find some one to assist me, and at last I succeeded. I was allowed two hours once in two weeks to go and return three miles. I could contrive no other way than to improve one of these opportunities, in which I was finally successful. I became acquainted with some persons who assisted slaves to escape by the underground railroad. They were colored people. I was to pretend going to church, and the man who was to assist and introduce me to the proper parties was to linger on the street opposite the house, and I was to follow at a short distance. On Sunday evening I begged leave to attend church, which was reluctantly granted if I completed all my work, which was no easy task. It appeared as if my mistress used every possible exertion to delay me from church, and I concluded that her old cloven-footed companion had impressed his intentions on her mind. Finally, when I was ready to start, my mistress took a notion to go out to ride, and desired me to dress her little boy, and then get ready for church. Extensive hoops were then worn, and as I had attached my whole wardrobe under mine by a cord around my waist, it required considerable dexterity and no small amount of maneuvering to hide the fact from my mistress. While attending to the child I had managed to stand in one corner of the room, for fear she might come in contact with me and thus discover that my hoops were not so elastic as they usually are. I endeavored to conceal my excitement by backing and edging very genteelly out of the door. I had nine pieces of clothing thus concealed on my person, and as the string which fastened them was small it caused me considerable discomfort. To my great satisfaction I at last passed into the street, and my master and mistress drove down the street in great haste and were soon out of sight. I saw my guide patiently awaiting me. I followed him at a distance until we arrived at the church, and there met two young ladies, one of whom handed me a pass and told me to follow them at a square's distance. It was now twilight. There was a company of soldiers about to take passage across the ferry, and I followed. I showed my pass, and proceeded up the stairs on the boat. While thus ascending the stairs, the cord which held my bundle of clothing broke, and my feet became entangled in my wardrobe, but by proceeding, the first step released one foot and the next the other. This was observed only by a few soldiers, who were too deeply engaged in their own affairs to interfere with mine. I seated myself in a remote corner of the boat, and in a few moments I landed on free soil for the first time in my life, except when hurled through Albany and Springfield at the time of our capture. I was now under my own control. The cars were waiting in Jefferson City for the passengers for Indianapolis, where we arrived about nine o'clock.

MATTIE IN INDIANAPOLIS—THE GLORY OF FREEDOM—
PRESIDENT LINCOLN'S REMAINS EXHIBITED

My first business, after my arrival at Indianapolis was to find a boarding place in which I at once succeeded, and in a few hours thereafter was at a place of service of my own choice. I had always been under the yoke of oppression, compelled to submit to its laws, and not allowed to advance a rod from the house, or even out of call, without a severe punishment. Now this con-

stant fear and restless yearning was over. It appeared as though
I had emerged into a new world, or had never lived in the old
one before. The people I lived with were Unionists, and became
immediately interested in teaching and encouraging me in my
literary advancement and all other important improvements,
which precisely met the natural desires for which my soul had
ever yearned since my earliest recollection. I could read a little,
but was not allowed to learn in slavery. I was obliged to pay
twenty-five cents for every letter written for me. I now began to
feel that as I was free I could learn to write, as well as others;
consequently Mrs. Harris, the lady with whom I lived, volunteered to assist me. I was soon enabled to write quite a legible
hand, which I find a great convenience. I would advise all,
young, middle aged or old, in a free country to learn to read and
write. If this little book should fall into the hands of one defi-
cient of the important knowledge of writing, I hope they will
remember the old maxim:—"Never too old to learn." Manage
your own secrets, and divulge them by the silent language of
your own pen. Had our blessed President considered it too
humiliating to learn in advanced years, our race would yet have
remained under the galling yoke of oppression. After I had been
with Mrs. Harris seven months, the joyful news came of the surrender of Lee's army and the capture of Richmond.

> Whilst the country's hearts were throbbing,
>   Filled with joy for victories won;
> Whilst the stars and stripes were waving
>   O'er each cottage, ship and dome,
> Came upon like winged lightning
>   Words that turned each joy to dread,
> Froze with horror as we listened:
>   Our beloved chieftain, Lincoln's dead.
>
> War's dark clouds has long held o'er us,
>   They have rolled their gloomy fold's away,
> And all the world is anxious, waiting
>   For that promised peaceful day.
> But that fearful blow inflicted,

Fell on his devoted head,
And from every town and hamlet
Came the cry our Chieftain's dead.

Weep, weep, O bleeding nation
For the patriot spirit fled,
All untold our country's future—
Buried with the silent dead.
God of battles, God of nations to our country send relief
Turn each lamentation into joy whilst we mourn our
    murdered chief.

On the Saturday after the assassination of the President
there was a meeting held on the Common, and a vote taken to
have the President's body brought through Indianapolis, for
the people to see his dear dead face. The vote was taken by
raising the hands, and when the question was put in favor of it
a thousand black hands were extended in the air, seemingly
higher and more visible than all the rest. Nor were their hands
alone raised, for in their deep sorrow and gloom they raised
their hearts to God, for well they knew that He, through mar-
tyred blood, had made them free. It was some time before the
remains reached Indianapolis, as it was near the last of the
route. The body was placed in the centre of the hall of the
State House, and we marched in by fours, and divided into two
on each side of the casket, and passed directly through the
Hall. It was very rainy,—nothing but umbrellas were to be
seen in any direction. The multitude were passing in and out
from eight o'clock in the morning till four o'clock in the afternoon. His body remained until twelve o'clock in the evening,
many distinguished persons visiting it, when amid the boom-
ing of cannon, it moved on its way to Springfield, its final rest-
ing-place. The death of the President was like an electric shock
to my soul. I could not feel convinced of his death until I gazed
upon his remains, and heard the last roll of the muffled drum
and the farewell boom of the cannon. I was then convinced
that though we were left to the tender mercies of God, we
were without a leader.

Gone, gone is our chieftain,
The tried and the true;
The grief of our nation the world never knew.
We mourn as a nation has never yet mourned;
The foe to our freedom more deeply has scorned.

In the height of his glory in manhood's full prime,
Our country's preserver through darkest of time;
A merciful being, whose kindness all shared
Shown mercy to others. Why was he not spared?

The lover of Justice, the friend of the slave,
He struck at oppression and made it a grave;
He spoke for our bond-men, and chains from them fell,
By making them soldiers they served our land well.

Because he had spoken from sea unto sea
Glad tidings go heavenward, our country is free,
And angels I'm thinking looked down from above,
With sweet smiles approving his great works of love.

His name with the honor forever will live,
And time to his laurels new lustre will give;
He lived so unselfish, so loyal and true,
That his deeds will shine brighter at every view.

Then honor and cherish the name of the brave,
The champion of freedom, the friend to the slave,
The far-sighted statesman who saw a fair end,
When north land and south land one flag shall defend.

Rest, rest, fallen chieftain, thy labors are o'er,
For thee mourns a nation as never before;
Farewell honored chieftain whom millions adore,
Farewell gentle spirit, whom heaven has won.

SISTER LOST—MOTHER'S ESCAPE

In two or three weeks after the body of the President was carried through, my sister made her escape, but by some means we

entirely lost trace of her. We heard she was in a free State. In three months my mother also escaped. She rose quite early in the morning, took my little brother, and arrived at my place of service in the afternoon. I was much surprised, and asked my mother how she came there. She could scarcely tell me for weeping, but I soon found out the mystery. After so many long years and so many attempts, for this was her seventh, she at last succeeded, and we were now all free. My mother had been a slave for more than forty-three years, and liberty was very sweet to her. The sound of freedom was music in our ears; the air was pure and fragrant; the genial rays of the glorious sun burst forth with a new lustre upon us, and all creation resounded in responses of praise to the author and creator of him who proclaimed life and freedom to the slave. I was overjoyed with my personal freedom, but the joy at my mother's escape was greater than anything I had ever known. It was a joy that reaches beyond the tide and anchors in the harbor of eternal rest. While in oppression, this eternal life-preserver had continually wafted her toward the land of freedom, which she was confident of gaining, whatever might betide. Our joy that we were permitted to mingle together our earthly bliss in glorious strains of freedom was indescribable. My mother responded with the children of Israel,—"The Lord is my strength and my song. The Lord is a man of war, and the Lord is his name." We left Indianapolis the day after my mother arrived, and took the cars at eleven o'clock the following evening for St. Louis, my native State. We were then free, and instead of being hurried along, bare headed and half naked, through cars and boats, by a brutal master with a bill of sale in his pocket, we were our own, comfortably clothed, and having the true emblems of freedom.

MOTHER'S MARRIAGE

It appeared to me that the city presented an entirely new aspect. The reader will remember that my mother was engaged to be married on the evening after we were kidnapped, and that Mr. Adams, her intended, had prepared the house for the occasion.

We now went in search of him. He had moved about five miles into the country. He had carefully preserved his furniture and was patiently awaiting our return. We were gone two years and four months. The clothing and furniture which we had collected were all destroyed. It was over a year after we left St. Louis before we heard from there. We went immediately from the cars to my aunt's, and from there went to Mr. Adams' residence and took him by surprise. They were married in a week after our return. My mother is comfortably situated on a small farm with a kind and affectionate companion, with whom she had formed an early acquaintance, and from whom she had been severed by the ruthless hand of Wrong; but by the divine hand of Justice they were now reunited forever.

MATTIE MEETS HER OLD MASTER— GOES TO SERVICE—IS SENT FOR BY HER STEP-FATHER IN LAWRENCE, MASS.

In a short time I had selected a place of service, and was improving my studies in a small way. The place I engaged was in the family where I was born, where my mother lived when my father Jackson made his escape. Although Mr. Canory's family were always kind to us, I felt a great difference between freedom and slavery. After I had been there a short time my step-father sent for me and my half brother to come to Lawrence. He had been waiting ever since the State was free, hoping to get some account of us. He had been informed, previously, that mother, in trying to make her escape, had perished by the way, and the children also, but he was never satisfied. He was aware that my aunt was permanently in St. Louis, as her master had given her family their freedom twenty years previous. She was formerly owned by Major Howe, harness and leather dealer, yet residing in St. Louis. And long may he live and his good works follow him and his posterity forever. My father well knew the deception of the rebels, and was determined to persevere until he had obtained a satisfactory account of his family. A gentleman moved directly from Lawrence to St. Louis, who made particular enquiries for us, and even called at my aunt's. We then heard directly from my father, and commenced correspondence. He had not heard directly from us since he made his escape, which was nine years. He had never heard of his little son who my mother was compelled by Mrs. Lewis to confine in a box. He was born eight months after he left. As soon as possible after my mother consented to let my little brother go to his father he sent means to assist us to make preparations for our journey to the North. At first he only sent for his little son. My mother was anxious about sending him alone. He was only eleven years old, and perfectly unused to traveling, and had never been away from his mother. Finally my father came to the conclusion that, as my mother had endured such extreme hardships and sufferings during the nine years he was not permitted to participate or render her any assistance, that it would afford him much pleasure in sending for us both, bearing our expenses and making us as comfortable as his means would allow. Money was sent us, and our kind friend, Mr. Howe, obtained our tickets and voluntarily assisted us in starting. We left for the North on Monday, April 9th, and arrived, safe and sound, on the 11th. We found my step-father's residence about six o'clock in the evening. He was not expecting us till the next day. Our meeting is better imagined than told. I cannot describe it. His little son was only two years old when he left, and I was eleven, and we never expected to meet him again this side of eternity. It was Freedom that brought us together. My father was comfortably situated in a nice white cottage, containing some eight rooms, all well furnished, and attached to it was a fine garden. His wife, who is a physician, was absent, but returned on the following day. The people were kind and friendly. They informed me there was no other colored family in the city, but my step-mother was continually crowded with friends and customers without distinction. My step-mother had buried her only son, who returned from the war in a decline. The white friends were all in deep sympathy with them. I felt immediately at home among such kind and friendly people, and have never felt homesick, except when I think of my poor mother's farewell embrace when she accompanied us to the cars. As soon as my step-

mother had arrived, and our excitement was over, they commenced calculating upon placing me in the Sabbath school at
the church where my mother belonged. On the next Sabbath I
accompanied her and joined the Sabbath school, she occupying
a side seat about middle way up the house. I was not reminded
of my color except by an occasional loafer or the Irish, usually
the colored man's enemy. I was never permitted to attend a
white church before, or ride in any public conveyance without
being placed in a car for the especial purpose; and in the street
cars we were not permitted to ride at all, either South or West.
Here I ride where I please, without the slightest remark, except
from the ignorant. Many ask me if I am contented. They can
imagine by the above contrast. My brother and myself entered
the public school, and found a host of interested friends and
formed many dear acquaintances whom I shall never forget.
After attending school a month the term closed. I advanced in
my studies as fast as could be expected. I never attended school
but one month before. I needed more attention than my kind
teacher could possibly bestow upon me, encumbered as she was
by so many small children. Mother then proposed my entering
some select school and placing myself entirely under its discipline and influence. I was much pleased with the idea, but as
they had already been to so much expense for me, I could not
wish to place them under any heavier contribution. I had previously told my step-mother my story, and how often my own
mother had wished she could have it published. I did not imagine she could find time to write and arrange it, but she immediately proposed writing and publishing the entire story, by the
sale of which I might obtain the aid towards completing my
studies. I am glad I came to the old Bay State, the people of
which the rebels hate with an extreme hatred. I found it just
such a place as I had imagined by the appearance of the soldiers
and the kindness they manifested.

> New England, that blessed land,
> All in a happy Union band;
> They with the needy share their bread
> And teach the weak the Word of God.

We never heard from my sister Hester, who made her escape from Kentucky, except when she was on the cars, though we have no doubt she succeeded in gaining her freedom.

SUMMARY

On my return to St. Louis I met my old master, Lewis, who strove so hard to sell us away that he might avoid seeing us free, on the street. He was so surprised that before he was aware of it he dropped a bow. My mother met Mrs. Lewis, her old mistress, with a large basket on her arm, trudging to market. It appeared she had lived to see the day when her children had to wait upon themselves, and she likewise. The Yankees had taken possession, and her posterity were on an equality with the black man. Mr. Lewis despised the Irish, and often declared he would board at the hotel before he would employ Irish help, but he now has a dissipated Irish cook. When I was his slave I was obliged to keep away every fly from the table, and not allow one to light on a person. They are now compelled to brush their own flies and dress themselves and children. Mr. Lewis' brother Benjamin was a more severe slave master than the one who owned me. He was a tobacconist and very wealthy. As soon as the war commenced he turned Unionist to save his property. He was very severe in his punishments. He used to extend his victim, fastened to a beam, with hands and feet tied, and inflict from fifty to three hundred lashes, laying their flesh entirely open, then bathe their quivering wounds with brine, and, through his nose, in a slow rebel tone he would tell them "You'd better walk a fair chalk line or else I'll give yer twice as much." His former friends, the guerrillas, were aware he only turned Union to save his cash, and they gave those persons he had abused a large share of his luxury. They then, in the presence of his wife and another distinguished lady, tortured him in a most inhuman manner. For pretending Unionism they placed him on a table and threatened to dissect him alive if he did not tell them where he kept his gold. He immediately informed them. They then stood him against the house and fired over his head. From that, they changed his position by turning him upside down, and raising him two feet from the floor, letting him dash his head against the floor until his skull was fractured, after which he lingered awhile and finally died. There was a long piece published in the paper respecting his repentance, benevolence, &c. All the slaves who ever lived in his family admit the Lord is able to save to the uttermost. He saved the thief on the cross, and perhaps he saved him.

When I made my escape from slavery I was in a query how I was to raise funds to bear my expenses. I finally came to the conclusion that as the laborer was worthy of his hire, I thought my wages should come from my master's pocket. Accordingly I took twenty-five dollars. After I was safe and had learned to write, I sent him a nice letter, thanking him for the kindness his pocket bestowed to me in time of need. I have never received any answer to it.

When I complete my education, if my life is spared, I shall endeavor to publish further details of our history in another volume from my own pen.

CHRISTIANITY

Christianity is a system claiming God for its author, and the welfare of man for its object. It is a system so uniform, exalted and pure, that the loftiest intellects have acknowledged its influence, and acquiesced in the justness of its claims. Genius has bent from his erratic course to gather fire from her altars, and pathos from the agony of Gethsemane and the sufferings of Calvary. Philosophy and science have paused amid their speculative researches and wonderous revelations, to gain wisdom from her teachings and knowledge from her precepts. Poetry has culled her fairest flowers and wreathed her softest, to bind her Author's "bleeding brow." Music has strung her sweetest lyres and breathed her noblest strains to celebrate His fame; whilst Learning has bent from her lofty heights to bow at the lowly cross. The constant friend of man, she has stood by him in his hour of greatest need. She has cheered the prisoner in his cell, and strengthened the martyr at the stake. She has nerved the frail and sinking heart of woman for high and holy deeds. The worn and weary have rested their fainting heads upon her bosom, and gathered strength from her words and courage from her counsels. She has been the staff of decrepit age, and the joy of manhood in its strength. She has bent over the form of lovely childhood, and suffered it to have a place in the Redeemer's arms. She has stood by the bed of the dying, and unveiled the glories of eternal life; gilding the darkness of the tomb with the glory of the resurrection.

Christianity has changed the moral aspect of nations. Idolatrous temples have crumbled at her touch, and guilt owned its deformity in her presence. The darkest habitations of earth have been irradiated with heavenly light, and the death shriek of immolated victims changed for ascriptions of praise to God and the Lamb. Envy and Malice have been rebuked by her contented look, and fretful Impatience by her gentle and resigned manner.

At her approach, fetters have been broken, and men have risen redeemed from dust, and freed from chains. Manhood has learned its dignity and worth, its kindred with angels, and alliance to God.

To man, guilty, fallen and degraded man, she shows a fountain drawn from the Redeemer's veins; there she bids him wash and be clean. She points him to "Mount Zion, the city of the living God, to an innumerable company of angels, to the spirits of just men made perfect, and to Jesus the Mediator of the new Covenant," and urges him to rise from the degradation of sin, renew his nature and join with them. She shows a pattern so spotless and holy, so elevated and pure, that he might shrink from it discouraged, did she not bring with her a promise from the lips of Jehovah, that he would give power to the faint, and might to those who have no strength. Learning may bring her ample pages and her ponderous records, rich with the spoils of every age, gathered from every land, and gleaned from every source. Philosophy and science may bring their abstruse researches and wonderous revelations—Literature her elegance, with the toils of the pen, and the labors of the pencil—

but they are idle tales compared to the truths of Christianity. They may cultivate the intellect, enlighten the understanding, give scope to the imagination, and refine the sensibilities; but they open not, to our dim eyes and longing vision, the land of crystal founts and deathless flowers. Philosophy searches earth; Religion opens heaven. Philosophy doubts and trembles at the portals of eternity; Religion lifts the veil, and shows us golden streets, lit by the Redeemer's countenance, and irradiated by his smile. Philosophy strives to reconcile us to death; Religion triumphs over it. Philosophy treads amid the pathway of stars, and stands a delighted listener to the music of the spheres; but Religion gazes on the glorious palaces of God, while the harpings of the blood-washed, and the songs of the redeemed, fall upon her ravished ear. Philosophy has her place; Religion her important sphere; one is of importance here, the other of infinite and vital importance both here and hereafter.

Amid ancient lore the Word of God stands unique and pre-eminent. Wonderful in its construction, admirable in its adaptation, it contains truths that a child may comprehend, and mysteries into which angels desire to look. It is in harmony with that adaptation of means to ends which pervades creation, from the polypus tribes, elaborating their coral homes, to man, the wondrous work of God. It forms the brightest link of that glorious chain which unites the humblest work of creation with the throne of the infinite and eternal Jehovah. As light, with its infinite particles and curiously blended colors, is suited to an eye prepared for the alterations of day; as air, with its subtle and invisible essence, is fitted for the delicate organs of respiration; and, in a word, as this material world is adapted to man's physical nature; so the word of eternal truth is adapted to his moral nature and mental constitution. It finds him wounded, sick and suffering, and points him to the balm of Gilead and the Physician of souls. It finds him stained by transgressions and defiled with guilt, and directs him to the "blood that cleanseth from all unrighteousness and sin." It finds him athirst and faint, pining amid the deserts of life, and shows him the wells of salvation and the rivers of life. It addresses itself to his moral and spiritual nature, makes provision for his wants and weaknesses, and meets his yearnings and aspirations. It is adapted to his mind in its earliest stages of progression, and its highest state of intellectuality. It provides light for his darkness, joy for his anguish, a solace for his woes, balm for his wounds, and heaven for his hopes. It unveils the unseen world, and reveals him who is the light of creation, and the joy of the universe, reconciled through the death of His Son. It promises the faithful a blessed re-union in a land undimmed with tears, undarkened by sorrow. It affords a truth for the living and a refuge for the dying. Aided by the Holy Spirit, it guides us through life, points out the shoals, the quicksands and hidden rocks which endanger our path, and at last leaves us with the eternal God for our refuge, and his everlasting arms for our protection.

From the Darkness Cometh the Light, or Struggles for Freedom

Dedication

To those who by their valor have made their name immortal, from whom we are daily learning the lessons of patriotism, in whom we respect the virtues of charity, patience and friendship as displayed towards the colored race and to those

"Whose deeds crowd History's pages
And Time's great volume make,"

is this little volume reverently dedicated—

THE GRAND ARMY OF THE REPUBLIC.

Preface

So many of my friends have urged me to give a short sketch of my varied life that I have consented, and herewith present it for the consideration of my readers. Those who were with me in the days of slavery will appreciate these pages, for though they cannot recur with any happiness to the now "shadowy past, or renew the unrenewable," the unaccountable longing for the aged to look backward and review the events of their youth will find an answering chord in this little book.

Those of you who have never suffered as we have, perhaps may suppose the case, and therefore accept with interest and sympathy the passages of life and character here portrayed and the lessons which should follow from them.

If there is a want of unity or coherence in this work, be charitable and attribute it to lack of knowledge and experience in literary acquirements. As this is a world of varied interests and many events, although we are each but atoms, it must be remembered, that we assist in making the grand total of all history, and therefore are excusable in making our affairs of importance to ourselves, and endeavoring to impress them on others. With this reason of my seeking your favor, I leave you to the perusal of my little tale.

L. A. D.

From the Darkness Cometh the Light,
or
Struggles for Freedom
Lucy A. Delaney

CHAPTER I

"Soon is the echo and the shadow o'er,
 Soon, soon we lie with lid-encumbered eyes
And the great fabrics that we reared before
 Crumble to make a dust to hide who dies."

In the year 18——, Mr. and Mrs. John Woods and Mr. and Mrs. Andrew Posey lived as one family in the State of Illinois. Living with Mrs. Posey was a little negro girl, named Polly Crocket, who had made it her home there, in peace and happiness, for five years. On a dismal night in the month of September, Polly, with four other colored persons, were kidnapped, and, after being securely bound and gagged, were put into a skiff and carried across the Mississippi River to the city of St. Louis. Shortly after, these unfortunate negroes were taken up the Missouri River and sold into slavery. Polly was purchased by a farmer. Thomas Botts, with whom she resided for a year, when, overtaken by business reverses, he was obliged to sell all he possessed, including his negroes.

Among those present on the day set apart for the sale was Major Taylor Berry, a wealthy gentleman who had travelled a long distance for the purpose of purchasing a servant girl for his wife. As was the custom, all the negroes were brought out and placed in a line, so that the buyers could examine their good points at leisure. Major Berry was immediately attracted by the bright and alert appearance of Polly, and at once negotiated with the trader, paid the price agreed upon, and started for home to present his wife with this flesh and blood commodity, which money could so easily procure in our vaunted land of freedom.

Mrs. Fanny Berry was highly pleased with Polly's manner and appearance, and concluded to make a seamstress of her. Major Berry had a mulatto servant, who was as handsome as an Apollo, and when he and Polly met each other, day after day, the natural result followed, and in a short time, with the full consent of Major Berry and his wife, were married. Two children were the fruit of this marriage, my sister Nancy and myself, Lucy A. Delaney.

While living in Franklin county, Major Berry became involved in a quarrel with some gentleman, and a duel was resorted to, to settle the difficulty and avenge some fancied insult. The major arranged his affairs and made his will, leaving his negroes to his wife during her life-time and at her death they were to be free; this was his expressed wish.

My father accompanied Major Berry to New Madrid, where the fatal duel was fought, and stayed by him until the end came, received his last sigh, his last words, and closed his dying eyes, and afterwards conveyed the remains of his best friend to the bereaved family with a sad heart. Though sympathizing deeply with them in their affliction, my father was much disturbed as to what disposition would be made of him, and after Major Berry was consigned with loving hands to his last resting place, these haunting thoughts obtruded, even in his sleeping hours.

A few years after, Major Berry's widow married Robert Wash, an eminent lawyer, who afterwards became Judge of the Supreme Court. One child was born to them, who, when she grew to womanhood, became Mrs. Francis W. Goode, whom I shall always hold in grateful remembrance as long as life lasts, and God bless her in her old age, is my fervent prayer for her kindness to me, a poor little slave girl!

We lived in the old "Wash" mansion some time after the marriage of the Judge, until their daughter Frances was born. How well I remember those happy days! Slavery had no horror then for me, as I played about the place, with the same joyful freedom as the little white children. With mother, father and sister, a pleasant home and surroundings, what happier child than I!

As I carelessly played away the hours, mother's smiles would fade away, and her brow contract into a heavy frown. I wondered much thereat, but the time came—ah! only too soon, when I learned the secret of her ever-changing face!

CHAPTER II

Mrs. Wash lost her health, and, on the advice of a physician, went to Pensacola, Florida, accompanied by my mother. There she died, and her body was brought back to St. Louis and there interred. After Mrs. Wash's death, the troubles of my parents and their children may be said to have really commenced.

Though in direct opposition to the will of Major Berry, my father's quondam master and friend, Judge Wash tore my father from his wife and children and sold him "way down South!"

Slavery! cursed slavery! what crimes has it invoked! and, oh! what retribution has a righteous God visited upon these traders in human flesh! The rivers of tears shed by us helpless ones, in captivity, were turned to lakes of of blood! How often have we cried in our anguish, "Oh! Lord, how long, how long?" But the handwriting was on the wall, and tardy justice came at last and avenged the woes of an oppressed race! Chickamauga, Shiloh, Atlanta and Gettysburgh, spoke in thunder tones! John Brown's body had indeed marched on, and we, the ransomed ones, glorify God and dedicate ourselves to His service, and acknowledge His greatness and goodness in rescuing us from such bondage as parts husband from wife, the mother from her children, aye, even the babe from her breast!

Major Berry's daughter Mary, shortly after, married H. S. Cox, of Philadelphia, and they went to that city to pass their honeymoon, taking my sister Nancy with them as waiting-maid. When my father was sold South, my mother registered a solemn vow that her children should not continue in slavery all their lives, and she never spared an opportunity to impress it upon us, that we must get our freedom whenever the chance offered. So here was an unlooked-for avenue of escape which presented much that was favorable in carrying out her desire to see Nancy a free woman. Having been brought up in a free State, mother had learned much to her advantage, which would have been impossible in a slave State, and which she now proposed to turn to account for the benefit of her daughter. So mother instructed my sister not to return with Mr. and Mrs. Cox, but to run away, as soon as chance offered, to Canada, where a friend of our mother's lived who was also a runaway slave, living in freedom and happiness in Toronto.

As the happy couple wandered from city to city, in search of pleasure, my sister was constantly turning over in her mind various plans of escape. Fortune finally favored Nancy, for on their homeward trip they stopped at Niagara Falls for a few days. In her own words I will describe her escape:

"In the morning, Mr. and Mrs. Cox went for a drive, telling me that I could have the day to do as I pleased. The shores of Canada had been tantalizing my longing gaze for some days, and I was bound to reach there long before my mistress returned. So I locked up Mrs. Cox's trunk and put the key under the pillow, where I was sure she would find it, and I made a strike for freedom! A servant in the hotel gave me all necessary information and even assisted me in getting away. Some kind of a festival was going on, and a large crowd was marching from the rink to the river, headed by a band of music. In such a motley throng I was unnoticed, but was trembling with fear of being detected. It seemed an age before the ferry boat arrived, which at last appeared, enveloped in a gigantic wreath of black smoke. Hastily I embarked, and as the boat stole away into the misty twilight and among crushing fields of ice, though the air was chill and gloomy, I felt the warmth of freedom as I neared the Canada shore. I landed, without question, and found my mother's friend with but little difficulty, who assisted me to get work and support myself. Not long afterwards, I married a prosperous farmer, who provided me with a happy home, where I brought my children into the world without the sin of slavery to strive against."

On the return of Mrs. Cox to St. Louis she sent for my mother and told her that Nancy had run away. Mother was very thankful, and in her heart arose a prayer of thanks-giving, but outwardly she pretended to be vexed and angry. Oh! the impenetrable mask of these poor black creatures! how much of joy, of sorrow, of misery and anguish have they hidden from their tormentors!

I was a small girl at that time, but remember how wildly mother showed her joy at Nancy's escape when we were alone together. She would dance, clap her hands, and, waving them above her head, would indulge in one of those weird negro melodies, which so charm and fascinate the listener.

Mrs. Cox commenced housekeeping on a grand and extended scale, having a large acquaintance, she entertained lavishly. My mother cared for the laundry, and I, who was living with a Mrs. Underhill, from New York, and was having rather good times, was compelled to go live with Mrs. Cox to mind the baby. My pathway was thorny enough, and though there may be no roses without thorns, I had thorns in plenty with no roses.

I was beginning to plan for freedom, and was forever on the alert for a chance to escape and join my sister. I was then twelve years old, and often talked the matter over with mother and canvassed the probabilities of both of us getting away. No schemes were too wild for us to consider! Mother was especially restless, because she was a free woman up to the time of her being kidnapped, so the injustice and weight of slavery bore more heavily upon her than upon me. She did not dare to talk it over with anyone for fear that they would sell her further down the river, so I was her only confidant. Mother was always planning and getting ready to go, and while the fire was burning brightly, it but needed a little more provocation to add to the flames.

CHAPTER III

Mrs. Cox was always very severe and exacting with my mother, and one occasion, when something did not suit her, she turned on mother like a fury, and declared, "I am just tired out

with the 'white airs' you put on, and if you don't behave differ-
ently, I will make Mr. Cox sell you down the river at once."

Although mother turned grey with fear, she presented a bold
front and retorted that "she didn't care, she was tired of that
place, and didn't like to live there, nohow." This so infuriated Mr.
Cox that he cried, "How dare a negro say what she liked or what
she did not like; and he would show her what he should do."

So, on the day following, he took my mother to an auction-
room on Main Street and sold her to the highest bidder, for five
hundred and fifty dollars. Oh! God! the pity of it! "In the home
of the brave and the land of the free," in the sight of the stars
and stripes—that symbol of freedom—sold away from her child,
to satisfy the anger of a peevish mistress!

My mother returned to the house to get her few belongings, and
straining me to her breast, begged me to be a good girl, that she
was going to run away, and would buy me as soon as she could.
With all the inborn faith of a child, I believed it most fondly, and
when I heard that she had actually made her escape, three weeks
after, my heart gave an exultant throb and cried, "God is good!"

A large reward was offered, the bloodhounds (curse them and
curse their masters) were set loose on her trail. In the day time
she hid in caves and the surrounding woods, and in the night
time, guided by the wondrous North Star, that blessed lodestone
of a slave people, my mother finally reached Chicago, where she
was arrested by the negro-catchers. At this time the Fugitive
Slave Law was in full operation, and it was against the law of the
whole country to aid and protect an escaped slave; not even a
drink of water, for the love of the Master, might be given, and
those who dared to do it (and there were many such brave
hearts, thank God!) placed their lives in danger.

The presence of bloodhounds and "nigger-catchers" in their
midst, created great excitement and scandalized the community.
Feeling ran high and hundreds of people gathered together and
declared that mother should not be returned to slavery; but
fearing that Mr. Cox would wreak his vengeance upon me, my
mother finally gave herself up to her captors, and returned to
St. Louis. And so the mothers of Israel have been ever slain
through their deepest affections!

After my mother's return, she decided to sue for her freedom, and for that purpose employed a good lawyer. She had ample testimony to prove that she was kidnapped, and it was so fully verified that the jury decided that she was a free woman, and papers were made out accordingly.

In the meanwhile, Miss Martha Berry had married Mr. Mitchell and taken me to live with her. I had never been taught to work, as playing with the babies had been my sole occupation; therefore, when Mrs. Mitchell commanded me to do the weekly washing and ironing, I had no more idea how it was to be done than Mrs. Mitchell herself. But I made the effort to do what she required, and my failure would have been amusing had it not been so appalling. In those days filtering was unknown and the many ways of clearing water were to me an unsolved riddle. I never had to do it, so it never concerned me how the clothes were ever washed clean.

As the Mississippi water was even muddier than now, the results of my washing can be better imagined than described. After soaking and boiling the clothes in its earthy depths, for a couple of days, in vain attempt to get them clean, and rinsing through several waters, I found the clothes were getting darker and darker, until they nearly approximated my own color. In my despair, I frantically rushed to my mother and sobbed out my troubles on her kindly breast. So in the morning, before the white people had arisen, a friend of my mother came to the house and washed out the clothes. During all this time, Mrs. Mitchell was scolding vigorously, saying over and over again, "Lucy, you do not want to work, you are a lazy, good-for-nothing nigger!" I was angry at being called a nigger, and replied, "You don't know nothing, yourself, about it, and you expect a poor ignorant girl to know more than you do yourself; if you had any feeling you would get somebody to teach me, and then I'd do well enough."

She then gave me a wrapper to do up, and told me if I ruined that as I did the other clothes, she would whip me severely. I answered, "You have no business to whip me. I don't belong to you."

My mother had so often told me that she was a free woman and that I should not die a slave, I always had a feeling of independence, which would invariably crop out in these encounters with my mistress; and when I thus spoke, saucily, I must confess, she opened her eyes in angry amazement and cried:

"You *do* belong to me, for my papa left you to me in his will, when you were a baby, and you ought to be ashamed of yourself to talk so to one that you have been raised with; now, you take that wrapper, and if you don't do it up properly, I will bring you up with a round turn."

Without further comment, I took the wrapper, which was too handsome to trust to an inexperienced hand, like Mrs. Mitchell very well knew I was, and washed it, with the same direful results as chronicled before. But I could not help it, as heaven is my witness. I was entirely and hopelessly ignorant! But of course my mistress would not believe it, and declared over and over again, that I did it on purpose to provoke her and show my defiance of her wishes. In vain did I disclaim any such intentions. She was bound to carry out her threat of whipping me.

I rebelled against such government, and would not permit her to strike me; she used shovel, tongs and broomstick in vain, as I disarmed her as fast as she picked up each weapon. Infuriated at her failure, my opposition and determination not to be whipped, Mrs. Mitchell declared she would report me to Mr. Mitchell and have him punish me.

When her husband returned home, she immediately entered a list of complaints against me as long as the moral law, including my failure to wash her clothes properly, and her inability to break my head for it; the last indictment seemed to be the heaviest she could bring against me. I was in the shadow of the doorway as the woman raved, while Mr. Mitchell listened patiently until the end of his wife's grievances reached an appeal to him to whip me with the strength that a man alone could possess.

Then he declared, "Martha, this thing of cutting up and slashing servants is something I know nothing about, and positively will not do. I don't believe in slavery, anyhow; it is a curse on this land, and I wish we were well rid of it."

"Mr. Mitchell, I will not have that saucy baggage around this house, for if she finds you won't whip her, there will be no living with her, so you shall just sell her, and I insist upon it."

"Well, Martha," he answered, "I found the girl with you when we were married, and as you claim her as yours, I shall not interpose any objections to the disposal of what you choose to call your property, in any manner you see fit, and I will make arrangements for selling her at once."

I distinctly overheard all that was said, and was just as determined not to be sold as I was not to be whipped. My mother's lawyer had told her to caution me never to go out of the city, if, at any time, the white people wanted me to go, so I was quite settled as to my course, in case Mr. Mitchell undertook to sell me.

Several days after this conversation took place, Mrs. Mitchell, with her baby and nurse, Lucy Wash, made a visit to her grandmother's, leaving orders that I should be sold before her return; so I was not surprised to be ordered by Mr. Mitchell to pack up my clothes and get ready to go down the river, for I was to be sold that morning, and leave, on the steamboat Alex. Scott, at 3 o'clock in the afternoon.

"Can't I go see my mother, first?" I asked.

"No," he replied, not very gently, "there is no time for that, you can see her when you come back. So hurry up and get ready, and let us have no more words about it!"

How I did hate him! To hear him talk as if I were going to take a pleasure trip, when he knew that if he sold me South, as he intended, I would never see my dear mother again.

However, I hastily ran up stairs and packed my trunk, but my mother's injunction, "never to go out of the city," was ever present in my mind.

Mr. Mitchell was Superintendent of Indian Affairs, his office being in the dwelling house, and I could hear him giving orders to his clerk, as I ran lightly down the stairs, out of the front door to the street, and with fleet foot, I skimmed the road which led to my mother's door, and, reaching it, stood trembling in every limb with terror and fatigue.

I could not gain admittance, as my mother was away to work and the door was locked. A white woman, living next door, and who was always friendly to mother, told me that she would not return until night. I clasped my hands in despair and cried, "Oh!

the white people have sold me, and I had to run away to keep from being sent down the river."

This white lady, whose name I am sorry I cannot remember, sympathized with me, as she knew my mother's story and had written many letters for her, so she offered me the key of her house, which, fortunately, fitted my mother's door, and I was soon inside, cowering with fear in the darkness, magnifying every noise and every passing wind, until my imagination had almost converted the little cottage into a boat, and I was steaming down South, away from my mother, as fast as I could go.

Late at night mother returned, and was told all that had happened, and after getting supper she took me to a friend's house for concealment, until the next day.

As soon as Mr. Mitchell had discovered my unlooked-for departure, he was furious, for he did not think I had sense enough to run away; he accused the coachman of helping me off, and, despite the poor man's denials, hurried him away to the calaboose and put him under the lash, in order to force a confession. Finding this course unavailing, he offered a reward to the negro catchers, on the same evening, but their efforts were equally fruitless.

CHAPTER IV

On the morning of the 8th of September, 1842, my mother sued Mr. D. D. Mitchell for the possession of her child, Lucy Ann Berry. My mother, accompanied by the sheriff, took me from my hiding-place and conveyed me to the jail, which was located on Sixth Street, between Chestnut and Market, where the Laclede Hotel now stands, and there met Mr. Mitchell, with Mr. H. S. Cox, his brother in-law.

Judge Bryant Mullanphy read the law to Mr. Mitchell, which stated that if Mr. Mitchell took me back to his house, he must give bond and security to the amount of two thousand dollars, and furthermore, I should not be taken out of the State of Missouri until I had a chance to prove my freedom. Mr. H. S.

Cox became his security and Mr. Mitchell gave bond accordingly, and then demanded that I should be put in jail.

"Why do you want to put that poor young girl in jail?" demanded my lawyer. "Because," he retorted, "her mother or some of her crew might run her off, just to make me pay the two thousand dollars; and I would like to see her lawyer, or any other man, in jail, that would take up a d—— nigger case like that."

"You need not think, Mr. Mitchell," calmly replied Mr. Murdock, "because my client is colored that she has no rights, and can be cheated out of her freedom. She is just as free as you are, and the Court will so decide it, as you will see."

However, I was put in a cell, under lock and key, and there remained for seventeen long and dreary months, listening to the

"—— foreign echoes from the street,
Faint sounds of revel, traffic, conflict keen—
And, thinking that man's reiterated feet
Have gone such ways since e'er the world has been,
I wondered how each oft-used tone and glance
Retains its might and old significance."

My only crime was seeking for that freedom which was my birthright! I heard Mr. Mitchell tell his wife that he did not believe in slavery, yet, through his instrumentality, I was shut away from the sunlight, because he was determined to prove me a slave, and thus keep me in bondage. Consistency, thou art a jewel!

At the time my mother entered suit for her freedom, she was not instructed to mention her two children, Nancy and Lucy, so the white people took advantage of this flaw, and showed a determination to use every means in their power to prove that I was not her child.

This gave my mother an immense amount of trouble, but she had girded up her loins for the fight, and, knowing that she was right, was resolved, by the help of God and a good lawyer, to win my case against all opposition.

After advice by competent persons, mother went to Judge Edward Bates and begged him to plead the case, and, after fully considering the proofs and learning that my mother was a poor woman, he consented to undertake the case and make his charges only sufficient to cover his expenses. It would be well here to give a brief sketch of Judge Bates, as many people wondered that such a distinguished statesman would take up the case of an obscure negro girl.

Edward Bates was born in Belmont, Goochland county, Va., September, 1793. He was of Quaker descent, and inherited all the virtues of that peace-loving people. In 1812, he received a midshipman's warrant, and was only prevented from following the sea by the influence of his mother, to whom he was greatly attached. Edward emigrated to Missouri in 1814, and entered upon the practice of law, and, in 1816, was appointed prosecuting lawyer for the St. Louis Circuit. Toward the close of the same year, he was appointed Attorney General for the new State of Missouri, and in 1826, while yet a young man, was elected representative to congress as an anti-Democrat, and served one term. For the following twenty-five years, he devoted himself to his profession, in which he was a shining light. His probity and uprightness attracted to him a class of people who were in the right and only sought justice, while he repelled, by his virtues, those who traffic in the miseries or mistakes of unfortunate people, for they dared not come to him and seek counsel to aid them in their villainy.

In 1847, Mr. Bates was delegate to the Convention for Internal Improvement, held in Chicago, and by his action he came prominently before the whole country. In 1850, President Fillmore offered him the portfolio of Secretary of War, which he declined. Three years later, he accepted the office of Judge of St. Louis Land Court.

When the question of the repeal of the Missouri Compromise was agitated, he earnestly opposed it, and thus became identified with the "free labor" party in Missouri, and united with it, in opposition to the admission of Kansas under the Lecompton Constitution. He afterwards became a prominent antislavery man, and in 1859 was mentioned as a candidate for the presidency. He was warmly supported by his own State, and for a time it seemed that the opposition to Governor Seward might concentrate on him. In the National Republican Convention, 1860, he received forty-eight votes on the first ballot, but when it became apparent that Abraham Lincoln was the favorite, Mr. Bates withdrew his name. Mr. Lincoln appointed Judge Bates Attorney General, and while in the Cabinet he acted a dignified, safe and faithful part. In 1864, he resigned his office and returned to his home in St. Louis, where he died in 1869, surrounded by his weeping family.

> "—— loved at home, revered abroad.
> Princes and lords are but the breath of kings;
> 'An honest man's the noblest work of God.'"

On the 7th of February, 1844, the suit for my freedom began. A bright, sunny day, a day which the happy and care-free would drink in with a keen sense of enjoyment. But my heart was full of bitterness; I could see only gloom which seemed to deepen and gather closer to me as I neared the courtroom. The jailer's sister-in-law, Mrs. Lacy, spoke to me of submission and patience; but I could not feel anything but rebellion against my lot. I could not see one gleam of brightness in my future, as I was hurried on to hear my fate decided.

Among the most important witnesses were Judge Robert Wash and Mr. Harry Douglas, who had been an overseer on Judge Wash's farm, and also Mr. MacKeon, who bought my mother from H. S. Cox, just previous to her running away.

Judge Wash testified that "the defendant, Lucy A. Berry, was a mere infant when he came in possession of Mrs. Fannie Berry's estate, and that he often saw the child in the care of its reputed mother, Polly, and to his best knowledge and belief, he thought Lucy A. Berry was Polly's own child."

Mr. Douglas and Mr. MacKeon corroborated Judge Wash's statement. After the evidence from both sides was all in, Mr. Mitchell's lawyer, Thomas Hutchinson, commenced to plead. For one hour, he talked so bitterly against me and against my being in possession of my liberty that I was trembling, as if with ague, for I certainly thought everybody must believe him; indeed I almost believed the dreadful things he said, myself, and as I listened I closed my eyes with sickening dread, for I could just see myself floating down the river, and my heart-throbs seemed to be the throbs of the mighty engine which propelled me from my mother and freedom forever!

Oh! what a relief it was to me when he finally finished his harangue and resumed his seat! As I never heard anyone plead before, I was very much alarmed, although I knew in my heart that every word he uttered was a lie! Yet, how was I to make people believe? It seemed a puzzling question!

Judge Bates arose, and his soulful eloquence and earnest pleading made such an impression on my sore heart, I listened with renewed hope. I felt the black storm clouds of doubt and despair were fading away, and that I was drifting into the safe harbor of the realms of truth. I felt as if everybody *must* believe *him*, for he clung to the truth, and I wondered how Mr. Hutchinson could so lie about a poor defenseless girl like me.

Judge Bates chained his hearers with the graphic history of my mother's life, from the time she played on Illinois banks, through her trials in slavery, her separation from her husband, her efforts to become free, her voluntary return to slavery for the sake of her child, Lucy, and her subsequent efforts in securing her own freedom. All these incidents he lingered over step by step, and concluding, he said:

"Gentlemen of the jury, I am a slave-holder myself, but, thanks to the Almighty God, I am above the base principle of holding anybody a slave that has as good right to her freedom as this girl has been proven to have; she was free before she was born; her mother was free, but kidnapped in her youth, and sacrificed to the greed of negro traders, and no free woman can give birth to a slave child, as it is in direct violation of the laws of God and man!"

At this juncture he read the affidavit of Mr. A. Posey, with whom my mother lived at the time of her abduction; also affidavits of Mr. and Mrs. Woods, in corroboration of the previous facts duly set forth. Judge Bates then said:

"Gentleman of the jury, here I rest this case, as I would not want any better evidence for one of my own children. The testimony of Judge Wash is alone sufficient to substantiate the claim of Polly Crockett Berry to the defendant as being her own child."

The case was then submitted to the jury, about 8 o'clock in

the evening, and I was returned to the jail and locked in the cell which I had occupied for seventeen months, filled with the most intense anguish.

CHAPTER V

"There's a joy in every sorrow,
    There's a relief from every pain;
Though to-day 'tis dark to-morrow
    HE will turn all bright again."

Before the sheriff bade me good night he told me to be in readiness at nine o'clock on the following morning to accompany him back to court to hear the verdict. My mother was not at the trial. She had lingered many days about the jail expecting my case would be called, and finally when called to trial the dear, faithful heart was not present to sustain me during that dreadful speech of Mr. Hutchinson. All night long I suffered agonies of fright, the suspense was something awful, and could only be comprehended by those who have gone through some similar ordeal.

I had missed the consolation of my mother's presence, and I felt so hopeless and alone! Blessed mother! how she clung and fought for me. No work was too hard for her to undertake. Others would have flinched before the obstacles which confronted her, but undauntedly she pursued her way, until my freedom was established by every right and without a questioning doubt!

On the morning of my return to Court, I was utterly unable to help myself. I was so overcome with fright and emotion,—with the alternating feelings of despair and hope—that I could not stand still long enough to dress myself. I trembled like an aspen leaf; so I sent a message to Mrs. Lacy to request permission for me to go to her room, that she might assist me in dressing. I had done a great deal of sewing for Mrs. Lacy, for she had showed me much kindness, and was a good Christian. She gladly assisted me, and under her willing hands I was soon made

ready, and, promptly at nine o'clock, the sheriff called and
escorted me to the courthouse.

On our way thither, Judge Bates overtook us. He lived out a
short distance in the country, and was riding on horseback. He
tipped his hat to me as politely as if I were the finest lady in the
land, and cried out, "Good morning Miss Lucy, I suppose you
had pleasant dreams last night!" He seemed so bright and smil-
ing that I was inbued with renewed hope; and when he
addressed the sheriff with "Good morning Sir. I don't suppose
the jury was out twenty minutes were they?" and the sheriff
replied "oh! no, sir," my heart gave a leap, for I was sure that my
fate was decided for weal or woe.

I watched the judge until he turned the corner and desiring
to be relieved of suspense from my pent-up anxiety, I eagerly
asked the sheriff if I were free, but he gruffly answered that "he
didn't know." I was sure he did know, but was too mean to tell
me. How could he have been so flinty, when he must have seen
how worried I was.

At last the courthouse was reached and I had taken my seat in
such a condition of helpless terror that I could not tell one person from another. Friends and foes were as one, and vainly did
I try to distinguish them. My long confinement, burdened with
harrowing anxiety, the sleepless night I had just spent, the unaccountable absence of my mother, had brought me to an indescribable condition. I felt dazed, as if I were no longer myself. I
seemed to be another person—an on looker—and in my heart
dwelt a pity for the poor, lonely girl, with down-cast face, sitting
on the bench apart from anyone else in that noisy room. I found
myself wondering where Lucy's mother was, and how she would
feel if the trial went against her; I seemed to have lost all feeling about it, but was speculating what Lucy would do, and what
her mother would do, if the hand of Fate was raised against poor
Lucy! Oh! how sorry I did feel for myself!

At the sound of a gentle voice, I gathered courage to look
upward, and caught the kindly gleam of Judge Bates' eyes, as he
bent his gaze upon me and smilingly said, "I will have you discharged in a few minutes, Miss Lucy!"

Some other business occupied the attention of the Court, and when I had begun to think they had forgotten all about me, Judge Bates arose and said calmly, "Your Honor, I desire to have this girl, Lucy A. Berry, discharged before going into any other business."

Judge Mullanphy answered "Certainly!" Then the verdict was called for and rendered, and the jurymen resumed their places. Mr. Mitchell's lawyer jumped up and exclaimed:

"Your Honor, my client demands that this girl be remanded to jail. He does not consider that the case has had a fair trial, I am not informed as to what course he intends to pursue, but I am now expressing his present wishes?"

Judge Bates was on his feet in a second and cried: "For shame! is it not enough that this girl has been deprived of her liberty for a year and a half, that you must still pursue her after a fair and impartial trial before a jury, in which it was clearly proven and decided that she had every right to freedom? I demand that she be set at liberty at once!"

"I agree with Judge Bates," responded Judge Mullanphy, "and the girl may go!"

Oh! the overflowing thankfulness of my grateful heart at that moment, who could picture it? None but the good God above us! I could have kissed the feet of my deliverers, but I was too full to express my thanks, but with a voice trembling with tears I tried to thank Judge Bates for all his kindness.

As soon as possible, I returned to the jail to bid them all good-bye and thank them for their good treatment of me while under their care. They rejoiced with me in my good fortune and wished me much success and happiness in years to come.

I was much concerned at my mother's prolonged absence, and was deeply anxious to meet her and sob out my joy on her faithful bosom. Surely it was the hands of God which prevented mother's presence at the trial, for broken down with anxiety and loss of sleep on my account, the revulsion of feeling would have been greater than her over-wrought heart could have sustained.

As soon as she heard of the result, she hurried to meet me, and hand in hand we gazed into each others eyes and saw the light of freedom there, and we felt in our hearts that we could with one accord cry out: "Glory to God in the highest, and peace and good will towards men."

Dear, dear mother! how solemnly I invoke your spirit as I review these trying scenes of my girlhood, so long agone! Your patient face and neatly-dressed figure stands ever in the foreground of that checkered time; a figure showing naught to an on-looker but the common place virtues of an honest woman! Never would an ordinary observer connect those virtues with aught of heroism or greatness, but to me they are as bright rays as ever emanated from the lives of the great ones of earth, which are portrayed on historic pages—to me, the qualities of her true, steadfast heart and noble soul become "a constellation, and is tracked in Heaven straightway."

CHAPTER VI

After the trial was over and my mother had at last been awarded the right to own her own child, her next thought reverted to sister Nancy, who had been gone so long, and from whom we had never heard, and the greatest ambition mother now had was to see her child Nancy. So, we earnestly set ourselves to work to reach the desired end, which was to visit Canada and seek the long-lost girl. My mother being a first-class laundress, and myself an expert seamstress, it was easy to procure all the work we could do, and command our own prices. We found, as well as the whites, a great difference between slave and free labor, for while the first was compulsory, and, therefore, at the best, perfunctory, the latter must be superior in order to create a demand, and realizing this fully, mother and I expended the utmost care in our respective callings, and were well rewarded for our efforts.

By exercising rigid economy and much self-denial, we, at last, accumulated sufficient to enable mother to start for Canada, and oh! how rejoiced I was when that dear, overworked mother approached the time, when her hard-earned and long-deferred holiday was about to begin. The uses of adversity is a worn theme, and in it there is much of weak cant, but when it is considered how much of sacrifice the poverty-stricken must bear in order to procure the slightest gratification, should it not impress the thinking mind with amazement, how much of fortitude and patience the honest poor display in the exercise of self-denial! Oh! ye prosperous! prate of the uses of adversity as poetically as you please, we who are obliged to learn of them by bitter experience would greatly prefer a change of surroundings.

Mother arrived in Toronto two weeks after she left St. Louis, and surprised my sister Nancy, in a pleasant home. She had married a prosperous farmer, who owned the farm on which they lived, as well as some property in the city near by. Mother was indescribably happy in finding her child so pleasantly situated, and took much pleasure with her bright little grandchildren; and after a long visit, returned home, although strongly urged to remain the rest of her life with Nancy; but old people are like old trees, uproot them, and transplant to other scenes, they droop and die, no matter how bright the sunshine, or how balmy the breezes.

On her return, mother found me with Mrs. Elsie Thomas, where I had lived during her absence, still sewing for a livelihood. Those were the days in which sewing machines were unknown, and no stitching or sewing of any description was allowed to pass muster, unless each stitch looked as if it were a part of the cloth. The art of fine sewing was lost when sewing machines were invented, and though doubtless they have given women more leisure, they have destroyed that extreme neatness in the craft, which obtained in the days of long ago.

Time passed happily on with us, with no event to ruffle life's peaceful stream, until 1845, when I met Frederick Turner, and in a few short months we were made man and wife. After our marriage, we removed to Quincy, Ill., but our happiness was of short duration, as my husband was killed in the explosion of the steamboat Edward Bates, on which he was employed. To my mind it seemed a singular coincidence that the boat which bore the name of the great and good man, who had given me the first joy of my meagre life—the precious boon of freedom—and that his namesake should be the means of weighting me with my first great sorrow; this thought seemed to reconcile me to my grief, for that name was ever sacred, and I could not speak it without reverence.

The number of killed and wounded were many, and they were distributed among friends and hospitals; my husband was carried to a friend's, where he breathed his last. Telegraphs were wanting in those times, so days passed before this wretched piece of news reached me, and there being no railroads, and many delays, I reached the home of my friend only to be told that my husband was dead and buried. Intense grief was mine, and my repining worried mother greatly; she never believed in fretting about anything that could not be helped. My only consolation from her was, "Cast your burden on the Lord. *My* husband is down South, and I don't know where he is; he may be dead; he may be alive; he may be happy and comfortable; he may be kicked, abused and half-starved. *Your* husband, honey, is in heaven; and mine—God only knows where he is!"

In those few words, I knew her burden was heavier than mine, for I had been taught that there was hope beyond the grave, but hope was left behind when sold "down souf"; and so I resolved to conceal my grief, and devote myself to my mother, who had done so much and suffered so much for me.

We then returned to St. Louis, and took up the old life, minus the contentment which had always buoyed us up in our daily trials, and with an added sorrow which cast a sadness over us. But Time, the great healer, taught us patience and resignation, and once more we were

"Waiting when fortune sheds brightly her smile,
There always is something to wait for the while."

CHAPTER VII

Four years afterward, I became the wife of Zachariah Delaney, of Cincinnati, with whom I have had a happy married life, continuing forty-two years. Four children were born to us, and many were the plans we mapped out for their future, but two of our little girls were called from us while still in their childhood. My remaining daughter attained the age of twenty-two years, and left life behind, while the brightest of prospects was hers, and my son, in the fullness of a promising youth, at the age of twenty-four, "turned his face to the wall." So my cup of bitterness was full to the brim and overflowing; yet one consolation was always mine! Our children were born free and died free! Their childhood and my maternity were never shadowed with a thought of separation. The grim reaper did not spare them, but they were as "treasures laid up in heaven." Such a separation one could accept from the hand of God, with humble submission, "for He calleth His own!"

Mother always made her home with me until the day of her death; she had lived to see the joyful time when her race was made free, their chains struck off, and their right to their own flesh and blood lawfully acknowledged. Her life, so full of sorrow, was ended, full of years and surrounded by many friends, both black and white, who recognized and appreciated her sufferings and sacrifices and rejoiced that her old age was spent in freedom and plenty. The azure vault of heaven bends over us all, and the gleaming moonlight brightens the marble tablet which marks her last resting place, "to fame and fortune unknown," but in the eyes of Him who judgeth us, hers was a heroism which outvied the most famous.

* * * * * * *

I frequently thought of father, and wondered if he were alive or dead; and at the time of the great exodus of negroes from the South, a few years ago, a large number arrived in St. Louis, and were cared for by the colored people of that city. They were sheltered in churches, halls and private houses, until such time as they could pursue their journey. Methought, I will find him in this motley crowd, of all ages, from the crowing babe in its mother's arms, to the aged and decrepit, on whom the marks of slavery were still visible. I piled inquiry upon inquiry, until after long and persistent search, I learned that my father had always lived on the same plantation, fifteen miles from Vicksburg. I wrote to my father and begged him to come and see me and make his home with me; sent him the money, so he would be to no expense, and when he finally reached St. Louis, it was with great joy that I received him. Old, grizzled and gray, time had dealt hardly with him, and he looked very little like the dapper master's valet, whose dark beauty won my mother's heart.

Forty-five years of separation, hard work, rough times and heart longings, had perserveringly performed its work, and instead of a man bearing his years with upright vigor, he was made prematurely old by the accumulation of troubles. My sister Nancy came from Canada, and we had a most joyful reunion, and only the absence of our mother left a vacuum, which we deeply and sorrowfully felt. Father could not be persuaded to stay with us, when he found his wife dead; he longed to get back to his old associations of forty-five years standing, he felt like a stranger in a strange land, and taking pity on him, I urged him no more, but let him go, though with great reluctance.

❋ ❋ ❋ ❋ ❋ ❋ ❋

There are abounding in public and private libraries of all sorts, lives of people which fill our minds with amazement, admiration, sympathy, and indeed with as many feelings as there are people, so I can scarcely expect that the reader of these episodes of my life will meet with more than a passing interest, but as such I will commend it to your thought for a brief hour. To be sure, I am deeply sensible that this story, as written, is not a very striking performance, but I have brought you with me face to face with but only a few of the painful facts engendered by slavery, and the rest can be drawn from history. Just have patience a little longer, and I have done.

I became a member of the Methodist Episcopal Church in 1855; was elected President of the first colored society, called the "Female Union," which was the first ever organized exclusively for women; was elected President of a society known as the "Daughters of Zion"; was matron of "Siloam Court," No. 2, three years in succession; was Most Ancient Matron of the "Grand Court of Missouri," of which only the wives of Masons are allowed to become members. I am at present, Past Grand Chief Preceptress of the "Daughters of the Tabernacle and Knights of Tabor," and also was Secretary, and am still a member, of Col. Shaw Woman's Relief Corps, No. 34, auxiliary to the Col. Shaw Post, 343, Grand Army of the Republic.

Considering the limited advantages offered me, I have made

the best use of my time, and what few talents the Lord has bestowed on me I have not "hidden in a napkin," but used them for His glory and to benefit those for whom I live. And what better can we do than to live for others?

Except the deceitfulness of riches, nothing is so illusory as the supposition of interest we assume that our readers may feel in our affairs; but if this sketch is taken up for just a moment of your life, it may settle the problem in your mind, if not in others, "Can the negro race succeed, proportionately, as well as the whites, if given the same chance and an equal start?"

> "The hours are growing shorter for the millions who are
> toiling;
> And the homes are growing better for the millions yet to
> be;
> And we all shall learn the lesson, how that waste and sin
> are spoiling
> The fairest and the finest of a grand humanity.
>
> It is coming! it is coming! and men's thoughts are grow-
> ing deeper;
> They are giving of their millions as they never gave
> before;
> They are learning the new Gospel; man must be his
> brother's keeper,
> And right, not might, shall triumph, and the selfish rule
> no more."

FINIS.

A Slave Girl's Story

A Slave Girl's Story

Kate Drumgoold

CHAPTER I

Once a slave girl, I have endeavored to fill the pages with some of the most interesting thoughts that my mind is so full of, and not with something that is dry.

This sketch is written for the good of those that have written and prayed that the slaves might be a freed people, and have schools and books and learn to read and write for themselves; and the Lord, in His love for us and to us as a race, has ever found favor in His sight, for when we were in the land of bondage He heard the prayers of the faithful ones, and came to deliver them out of the Land of Egypt.

For God loves those that are oppressed, and will save them when they cry unto him, and when they put their trust in Him.

Some of the dear ones have gone to the better land, but this is one of the answers to their prayers.

We, as the Negro Race, are a free people, and God be praised for it. We as the Negro Race, need to feel proud of the race, and I for one do with all my heart and soul and mind, knowing as I do, for I have labored for the good of the race, that their children might be the bright and shining lights. And we can see the progress that we are making in an educational way in a short time, and I think that we should feel very grateful to God and those who are trying to help us forward. God bless such with their health, and heart full of that same love, that this world can not give nor taketh away.

There are many doors that are shut to keep us back as a race, but some are opened to us, and God be praised for those that are opened to the race, and I hope that they will be true to their trust and be of the greatest help to those that have given them a chance.

There are many that have lost their lives in the far South in trying to get an education, but there are many that have done well, and we feel like giving God all the praise.

I was born in Old Virginia, in or near the Valley, the other side of Petersburg, of slave parents, and I can just call to mind the time when the war began, for I was not troubled then about wars, as I was feeling as free as any one could feel, for I was sought by all of the rich whites of the neighborhood, as they all loved me, as noble whites will love a child, like I was in those days, and they would send for me if I should be at my play and have me to talk for them, and all of their friends learned to love me and send me presents, and I would stand and talk and preach for some time for them.

My dear mother was sold at the beginning of the war, from all of her little ones, after the death of the lady that she belonged to, and who was so kind to my dear mother and all of the rest of the negroes of the place; and she never liked the idea of holding us as slaves, and she always said that we were all that she had on the earth to love; and she did love me to the last.

The money that my mother was sold for was to keep the rich man from going to the field of battle, as he sent a poor white man in his stead, and should the war end in his favor, the poor white man should have given to him one negro, and that would fully pay for all of his service in the army. But my God moves in a way unknown to men, and they can never understand His ways, for He can plant His footsteps on the North, the South, the East, the West, and outride any man's ideas; and how wonderful are all of his ways. And if we, as a race, will only put our trust in Him, we shall gain the glorious victory, and be a people whose God is the God of all this broad earth, and may we humble ourselves before Him and call Him, Blessed.

I told you that my white mother did not like the idea of calling us her slaves, and she always prayed God that I should never know what slavery was, for she said I was never born to serve as did the slaves of some of the people that owned them.

And God, in His love for me and to me, never let me know of it, as did some of my own dear sisters, for some of them were hired out after the old home was broken up.

My mother was sold at Richmond, Virginia, and a gentleman bought her who lived in Georgia, and we did not know that she was sold until she was gone, and the saddest thought was to me to know which way she had gone, and I used to go outside and look up to see if there was anything that would direct me, and I saw a clear place in the sky, and it seemed to me the way she had gone, and I watched it three and a half years, not knowing what that meant, and it was there the whole time that mother was gone from her little ones.

On one bright Sunday I asked my older sister to go with me for a nice walk and she did so, for she was the one that was so kind to the rest of us—and we saw some sweet flowers on the wayside and we began to have delight in picking them, when all at once I was led to leave her alone with the flowers and to go where I could look up at that nice, clear spot, and as I wanted to get as near to it as I could, I got on the fence, and as I looked that way I saw a form coming to me that looked like my dear mother's, and calling to my sister Frances to come at once and see if that did not look like my dear mother, and she came to us, so glad to see us, and to ask after her baby that she was sold from that was only six weeks old when she was taken from it; and I would that the whole world could have seen the joy of a mother and her two girls on that heaven-made day—a mother returning back to her own once more, a mother that we did not know that we should ever see her face on this earth more. And mother, not feeling good over the past events, had made up her mind that she would take her children to a part of this land where she thought that they would never be in bondage any more on this earth.

So she sought out the head man that was placed there by the North to look after the welfare of lately emancipated negroes of the South, to see that they should have their rights as a freed people.

This gentleman's name was Major Bailley, who was a gentleman of the highest type, and it was this loving man that sent my dear mother and her ten little girls on to this lovely city, and the same time he informed the people of Brooklyn that we were on the way and what time we should reach there; and it seemed as though the whole city were out to meet us. And as God would have it, six of us had homes on that same day, and the people had their carriages there to take us to our new homes.

This God-sent blessing was of a great help to mother, as she could get the money to pay her rent, which was ten dollars per month, and God bless those of my sisters who could help mother to care for her little ones, for they had not been called home then, and God be praised for all that we have ever did for her love and comfort while she kept house.

The subject was only a few years old, when she saw her heart so fixed that she could not leave me at my mother's any longer, so she took me to be her own dear, loving child, to eat, drink, sleep and to go wherever she went, if it was for months, or even years; I had to be there as her own and not as a servant, for she did not like that, but I was there as her loving child for her to care for me, and everything that I wanted I had; truly do I feel grateful to my Heavenly Father for all of those blessings that came to me in the time that I needed so much of love and care.

This dear lady, Mrs. Bettie House, my white mother, died at the beginning of the war and then the time came for poor me to go to my own dear mother again for awhile, and soon the time came for us to be parted asunder, where we did not see one another any more until after the war of 1865. And we all thought that mother was dead, for we did not hear any tidings of her after she had reached the far South.

I shall never forget that lovely Sunday morning when I saw my dear mother returning again to her own native home and her own dear ones once more, but mother would not go to the house with us, as she did not want to take the law in her own hands. So she told sister and I where she was stopping and told us to come to her after we had told the gentleman where we lived, and I went to him and told him that mother had come back and wanted to have us to come where she was staying. He, Mr. House, did not want us to go, and I took my oldest sister and marched out to go where mother was and he did not like that freedom, and he tried to find which way that we had gone to the place, but he did not find us, and we had been to the place where the people were that had homes, and that they would kill us at first sight, and that was all that I wanted to see, and I did not find one thing true of their sayings.

Mother now has to tell the gentleman where to find all of her own dear ones whom God in His love for had kept for her, and she should have been very grateful to Him that her life had been prolonged and all that she had left alive were still alive, awaiting for her to return, and finding that her children were all over in different places, and now she has to tell where to find them, through the help of the Lord. And when she had gone for them and was told that some of her own were dead, she said that she would go and dig up their bones; but they were not dead, as was said, and she sent the soldiers after them and sometimes they were told the same as mother was, and some of the little ones had to be sent for two or three times before they were brought. My oldest sister knew where they all were, so she could help to get the rest.

One of my sisters who lived at the same place where we were living was detained and the soldiers had go three times before they could get her, for they said that she had died since we had left, for I would not stay at the place as he, Mr. House, did not want us to go on Monday to see my mother, on whom I should look to, as she had come to claim her own. I told my oldest sister that we would leave, and my sister Annie was at one of Mr. House's sons, who found that we were going to see mother and she came with us, so that left three there yet; that was sister Lavinia and the baby, sister Rosa, and they let mother have the baby, as it was a sickly child; and she had to send there three times before she could get sister Lavinia, and the last time the soldiers, with horses, went, and the House's took off all of her clothing and put them into water to keep them from taking her, and they had to take blankets and wrap her in them, and bring her to mother, and she took sick from that time from the long ride, and getting cold she nearly died.

One they hid in the garden; one they put in the cellar, and so

these were hard times for mother and us, who were in the road
one night walking to find some place to get out of the rain and
let those wet garments get dried, for it was so dark that we could
not see a hand before us.

But after all the hard trials we reached this lovely city, where
there are those that love and fear God, and who love the souls
of the negro as well as those of the white, the red, the yellow or
brown races of the earth, for we have ever found some of the
people who do not forget us day or night in their prayers, that
God will send a blessing to us as a race.

To my story of a life of slavery:

My dear mother had a dear husband that she was sold from
also, and he, not knowing that he should ever see my mother any
more, as the times were then, he waited for a while and then he
found him another wife, and when mother came and found that
he was married to another she tried to get him, but she could do
nothing about it; so having to leave him behind to look after the
last one and her family, although it seemed hard for her to do so.

My mother had a large family to take care of, but the Lord
was good to her and helped her, for she had laid some of them
away, and then there were ten little girls to care for. My brother
was lost to us and to mother also, as he was sent to the war to do
service for his owner, and we did not know if he was alive or not,
and he was my mother's only boy, as this is a girl family that you
do not see or hear of every day, for that made seventeen girls to
have battle through life had they all have lived to this time.

CHAPTER II

My mother did not know where my brother was before she was
sold, for we heard that he had tried to get over to the Northern
side and had been taken to Richmond, Va., and put into Castle
Thunder, and that was the last that we heard of him during the
war. When, to our surprise, we were on our way North we
learned that he was going to school; that the Northern people
had teachers there in the South to teach them to read and to
write; and he learning that we had gone North made himself

ready and came on, but he did not know where to find us, so getting a place to work, and the same time telling those that he worked for that his people were here somewhere, they found mother and got her to go to the place where he was, and sure enough there was her dead and lost boy, and the joy and love that came to that dear, loving mother and her only son on that day will never be known on this side of the grave, as they have both gone to the land of the blest, for my brother never used any bad language in his life, and when he took the Lord for his own, it was his meat and his drink to live for Him and to follow where He led, and he died a true child of the King.

A few years later and mother's name was enrolled in the Lambs' Book of Life, for she gladly answered to the roll call and fell asleep in the arms of Jesus.

Well, my first place was in Adelphi street, with a family by the name of Hammond, and I was there to help do the work, and when they found that I liked to work so well they wanted me to do so much that I left that place and got me another, for I did not get out to church or to Sunday-school, and that was not the way that I had been trained, for when I was three years old my white mother had taken me to church with her on horseback.

Well, I said that I saw these children going to school on every week day but Saturdays and on Sundays to Sunday-school, and I there at work as if it were not the Lord's day, and I never shall like to work on that day as I was born on Sunday morning.

Well, I left there not knowing what to do, and a white lady took me in and told me to stay there until I could get another place, and I helped her girl on the next day to finish all of the work and I made ready to look for a place, and God did help me to find one and I shall never forget Him as long as I live, for that was with a fine family and they showed me love at once and I showed them love in return.

They were members of the Washington Avenue Baptist Church, and a more beloved family never lived. This was the Bailley family—Mr. and Mrs. Bailley, Miss Abbey Bailley, Mr. Bailley's sister, a young lady in her teens, Miss Ella Bailley, and a nice boy by the name of Johnny Bailley, and they were a nice family and they took me to church on Sunday morning and sent me to

Sunday-school in the afternoon with their children, and what a heaven it seemed to me from the place where I was living at first.

I shall always remember my dear white mother, of whom I spoke of in the first part, and whom I shall call your attention to in many more pages of this little Life Book, and shall always remember her with love and the kindest feeling. She was a member of the true Methodist Church and was never seen by her darling child from the House of God since I could remember, for I was with her at all times on the family horse, Kimble, and when I got large enough to ride alone she bought me a fine black that had all the metal that a horse could have, and his name was Charlie Engrum, and she paid a large price for him, and he was the grandest horse I ever saw, and it was my delight to be near a horse or horses when I was a child, for I did not have any fear of any kind of horse, and I would take a ride the first thing in the morning, even before I would have my breakfast, and my dear white mother would save it for me as she knew that I would have that ride first; for it always made her feel proud to see how well I had learned to ride, and she was the one that had taught me how to ride, for she had me on the horse when I was three years old and from that time until she went home to come out no more forever.

I was two and a half years, as near as I can remember, when my own slave mother's house was burned to the ground, and I shall never forget that Saturday night. My mother's husband had gone to a dance and mother was there alone with her little ones, and we all came near getting burned up. We were all asleep when I awoke and found the house in a blaze. I did not know enough or I was so much scared that I did not call to my mother, but I think that she heard me when I rolled out of the bed, and she was out of the bed quick as could be and getting the feather beds she threw them out of the door and got the children and threw them out, and she, finding that she did not have them all, said, "My God! I have not all of my little ones"; and she ran in the house to look and she found me under the bed, for I saw so much fire that I was getting out of it, and God be praised that I was saved from that fire, and I have not had the time to run after any fires since, for that fire was all the fire I want.

I had not to stay there then, for the time is near at hand when I shall go to my white mother's to live, for she is in Tennessee and will come home soon to be with her darling child; and when she shall start again I shall go, and now the times are all well for me as then, but the time has come that the Lord has called her away from her child to be with Him, and how could I live without her? And she was to leave her sick child there for her own mother to care for, and God will raise up friends in this lonely world to look after those that cry unto heaven, believing that He is a hearer of the true prayer. I shall always remember that Saturday afternoon when I was lying so sick when my dearly beloved white mother took so sick, and they had the doctor there for me, and he had to see after her the same time, and she was getting so much worse all the time and the doctor had not any hopes of her, and they took me from the room where she was, to a room upstairs and she had them to take me down to look at her once more. That was on Sunday and on Monday she heard the call to her to come up to that blessed land where she should be forever with the Lord and her dear husband.

What a glory it must be for those that have washed their robes and made them white in the blood of the Lamb.

I can call to mind when she the blessed one, that I call my white mother, went to get me some shoes and a fine hat, and the one that sold them told her, as she looked at a hat I wanted, that its price was twenty dollars, but I was not thinking of the prices then as I do now, and I cried to have that hat and did not want any of the others, and he told my white mother that was too much for to spend on a hat for me, but she told him nothing would cost too much for her to get for me, and she got that fine hat for me and he had his money; so you can see how much she loved me. And now that dear one is gone from me, and it seemed the dearest one on this earth, and I did not think then that I could have lived without her whom God had given to me for this world, but God, in His wonderful love for me and to me, raised up friends for me and helped me to find favor in the sight of all the people, for they seemed to love me for her sake, and I did not get well for a long time.

This subject came to this dear lady, Mrs. Bettie House, when but three years old, and from the day she came to that house she walked in her footsteps, for she, Mrs. House, could not move, but she was right in the way; and when she used to set me down for my play at certain times in the day, when she was going in her room for prayer, she would find me near before she was through; and if ever there was a loving woman she was one, and I owe my love to God for such a one as she was to care for me all of those nights of watching by my bed, while the angels watched from above to see that I should rise from that bed and live to be a woman that would live for God and bless His name in all the earth, knowing that I am tempted and tried on every hand. But trusting in His omnipotent power I shall reach the land of the blest where that dear one has gone to come out no more forever.

Well, to my story:

Dear public, hoping that this little life will be read with the greatest love for humanity, and I am sure that if you have any love for the God of heaven you can not fail to find a love for this book, and I hope you will find a fullness of joy in reading this life, for if your heart was like a stone you would like to read this little life.

I had many a hard spell of sickness since the death of this lady and the doctors said that I could not live beyond a certain time, but every time they said so Doctor Jesus said she shall live, for because I live she shall live also; and He came to me and laid His strong arm around me and raised me up by the power of His might, and to see the salvation of our God in the land of the living. And to-day I can praise His name for His wonderful love to the children of man.

I told you that my brother was the oldest child of eighteen and he was in his teens when he was sent to the war; and it was a great thing to him when he found himself in the hands of a people that were so kind and good to him and showing such love for him, after being knocked around by those he had been staying with, and it seemed like a heaven to him; and he did learn fast, and he felt so glad to learn to read and to write, and he would sit at nights when he was through with his daily toil and write, so that he could let some one look at it and see how well he was getting along, and I saw how anxious he was to get an education. I asked my lady to let him come there and wait on the table, and have time to go every day to school, and she did so, and he would go to No. 1 School to Mr. C. Dosey, and he did nicely in his studies, and God be praised that he had that much to take home with him, and I shall always feel glad that I gave him that much.

I was thinking of my dear brother when the news reached me that he was in this city, and I can never tell any one how glad that I was to see the only boy that my mother ever had, for we all loved him dearly, as he cared for all the rest of the children and it was no more than natural that we should; and my mother thought so much of him that she often would say if we were all boys she would not have to worry, for boys could do so much better than girls. But I think that she found that the girls were the best in her old age, for if one could not be near her the other would, and if there is a time in the life of a parent it is when they are helpless, and a boy is not any good to care for a sick parent and they have to go without care.

But God be praised for all of the love and honor that was bestowed on mother before she went home, for God has told us to honor our fathers and our mothers that their days may be long upon the land which the Lord, thy God, giveth thee; and we can not do them enough honor for the love and the all night watching that we have when we are babies, and if we have all of the love and care that I had, I am sure that a mother has her hands full; and when now I think of the care and the worry that it was to take care of my sick body, I can not help telling some one of it, that they may feel as grateful as I feel, for God did give them love for me, and if there is one that should feel grateful it is this feeble-bodied slave girl, for I was such a slave to sickness, and God was so good to raise me, even me, and I will say, praise His name.

I was telling you of my white mother being so true to the attendance in the services of God, and I only wish that you could have known her as I did, for she was more like one of the heavenly host than she was like us, who are such sinful creatures. Now, it seems like sometimes that we have not much love for the One who had so much love for us that He gave all the dear One, that He had to bring us to Himself, that we should taste of those joys which He has for those who have washed their robes and made them white in the Blood of the Lamb.

The Lord helped me to find love and favor with all after my white mother was gone from this earth, when I felt that I would soon follow the darling one to the blessed mansion; and I would look to see her come to me, and I went as soon as I was well to the house and lay on the steps, and it was not until we had left the dear old place before I could be kept from there; and I wish that the whole world could have seen how much she was like an angel, and I would to God she could see me to-day; it would do you good. Lord, lead me on day by day, and help my feeble life to be formed like her's, for when I think how she used to watch by my bed at nights, while the angels watched by my bed from on high to see that I should rise; and is not God the One that I should serve? And I love to serve Him and honor Him, for He is my all in all; for she has shown me how great her love was for me and all of humanity, and I love to think of her love and to know how wonderful it would be to see her sweet face on this green earth, and it does seem to me as if I could almost see her by thinking of her so much.

I have said that we came to this lovely city in the year of our Lord 1865, and in that year I went to live with a good family that were members of the church, where the Lord spoke peace to my soul, under the preaching of the Rev. David Moore, then the beloved leader of the noblest band of God's children on this earth, and a more beloved people never lived. They were always on the lookout for any strangers that might come in the church; and they soon found me out as I was a stranger in the Monday night meeting. The dear pastor came to me the first one, for he did not stop to think whether I was an African or what nation I had come from, but he saw in me a soul, and he wanted to find out if there was any room for Jesus to live or what I should do with Jesus, or what should I do for Him, who had done so much for me; and my poor heart was ready and waiting for some one to come to its rescue. It was then and there that I yielded my life and my all to the one that can save to the uttermost all that come unto Him by the Lord Jesus Christ.

I followed my Lord and Master in the Jordan in the year of our Lord 1866, and those sweet moments have never left me once. As the years go by they seem to be the more sweet to my sinful soul, and I am trying to wing my way to these bright mansions above, where I shall meet those dear ones who have gone before.

I have had some of the darkest days of my life while on this voyage of life, but when it is dark Jesus says, "Peace, be still and fear not, for I will pilot thee."

And then my heart can sing:

> "Jesus, Saviour, pilot me
> Over life's tempestuous sea,
> Unknown waves before me roll,
> Hiding rocks and treacherous shoals
> Chart and compass come from Thee,
> Jesus, Saviour, pilot me."

I know that He has led me through paths seen and unseen and has been my pilot, for we have been called to pass through many a dark trial, but God has been able for it all.

My dear mother had four of her children called home to heaven within a short time. Some of them left her for the land of love in the same month, and there seemed like nothing but God's displeasure on us, but it was God's love to us, for we know that they are safe from all harm and danger in this world of sin and distress. Some of them I never saw more after landing in this city, but I shall see them and know them when I shall have fought the blessed battle on this side, and the victory shall be on the Lord's side. Then I can sing with the angels above:

> "Crown Him, Crown Him, angels.
> Crown Him, Crown Him, King of Kings.
> Crown Him, Crown Him, angels.
> Crown Him, Crown Him, Crown the Saviour King of
> Kings."

What joy there will be to crown Him as our Heavenly King and to know that we are the inhabitants of that kingdom.

CHAPTER III

I was baptized by the Rev. David Moore, the pastor of the Washington Avenue Church, who is one of the best beloved ones on this earth, for he never overlooked me in the time that my soul needed the Lord Jesus Christ to save me from my sins and make me a child of the King, which makes me what I am to day. I bless God that he ever put it in my dear mother's mind to come to this place, for she was not a Christian, and the heaviest burden that I have carried was praying for one that was the head of the great family where she should have been a leader of her dear ones to the Lamb of God, that taketh away the sins of the world. But God be praised for a little one to lead so many, for of all the people of mothers there was not one that knew of this love of God, and how many were the souls given for me to work for. I told my mother that I had found Jesus and was going to follow Him. She said, "My child, you are too young, I am afraid that you will not hold out." And I said, "Mother, if I should look to myself I should fail, but I look to Jesus. I have given my life and He can hold me in the power of His might and can keep me from failing; so I can not go against your will, but I must follow Him, for you know how He has saved me from sickness so many times, and now the time has come for me to pay my vows unto Him for making me His own." I went forward in the way that He marked out for me and then to pray that she might be saved.

My grandma was almost one hundred years old, and when she heard that the Lord had saved me and that I was praying for her she saw her own sins and asked me to come on to visit all of my people, and I, getting ready, got my oldest sister to go with me. I found that the way was opened for work, as there we began the work, and they were looking to see something that they would never see in this world, and sweetly they were all brought to the Saviour. Grandma went home to carry the good news and some of the rest have gone with the same good news.

Later years some of my sisters came and some did not come. Then some got tired and went back to the world, but I have no joy like the joy there is in the Lord.

My dear mother found the peace in Jesus before she went to that land of song. When the Lord sent the death angel to call her name she was ready to answer, "Here am I ready to go in, to come out no more."

My mother left us on the 28th day of February, 1894, in the triumph of faith in the Lord Jesus Christ. What a blessed thought that I shall soon be with her on the other side of the river to help her "Crown Him Lord of all."

To my story:

The subject of this sketch, as I said, was born again under the preaching of Rev. David Moore, of the Washington Avenue Baptist Church, which is one of the noblest churches of this city, and it has some of the best people in it of any church in the world, for there is more done for those in need in other lands. When I became a member of that church I could not read in any book, for I did not know a letter. There was a gentleman in the church by the name of Mr. Lansberry, who finding that I was one of those that was going to learn, went to a store and bought me a First Reader and gave it to me, and I did not lose any of my time at nights. I went to the meetings every night and came back and got a lady, who was a sister of Mr. Bailley, to be my teacher, and sometimes she used to be so very sleepy that she could not keep her eyes open and I would shake her and say that my lesson was to be learned, and it was always well learned. Then I went to the Sunday-school to let my Sunday-school teacher hear it on Sundays, and he, Mr. Ward, always said that he was sure that I would learn so fast I would soon catch up with his Bible Class. It was not long before I could lay my Reader down and take my lessons in the Bible, and I can bless God for all of this, for the love and the kindness that I received of all that knew me was a token of His great love for me, and I know that He was near me all the time to bring me nearer to the Light. My mind was then fixed that I should some day go to school and I could not rest night or day I was so anxious to go to school; but my dear mother could not send me. She had poor health and no one to help her to take care of the younger children, and I had to work and do the best I could with my books, hoping that the time would come that I should see myself sitting in some school studying, the same time asking mother to let two of the other children go to school every day. She did let them go for awhile, but some one came and wanted her to let them go to work out again and she let them go out to work.

Well, I said that I would go to school some day, and they had a fine time laughing at my high ideas and I let them laugh all that they wanted to, but I worked hard and long to get the means that I might be able to go, as I said, to some pay school, where I could not be stopped at any time. When I was almost ready to leave for some school the smallpox took me, and I was laid aside for three or four years; that is, I was not well, and thought that my plans were all broken. I still trusted in God, for I knew that He would do all things for me as long as I put my trust in Him.

Well, as time rolled on I found myself improving slowly and I was then living with a dear, good lady by the name of Miss L. A. Pousland, who is one of the loveliest ladies that ever lived, for she loves me to-day as a mother, though she is in eightieth odd year and is doing well for an old lady.

We were living in South Oxford street when I took sick of the smallpox and she did not want me taken away from there, as she wanted to take care of me herself, but I felt that it would be too much for her to wait on me, so the doctor said that it was only a heavy cold that I had taken and would be all right in a week or so. But I knew that I had a fever of some kind, so I asked that I might go to my mother's house, and she sent for the carriage and I went home.

When I had reached my mother's I felt somewhat better, only to grow worse all the time, and my eyes getting so that I could not see when it was day or night. I had a nurse that knew all about the disease and a good doctor that the city health doctor let take charge of the case after he had been out there to see me: and knowing that the case was taking, that no one should get it he let me remain at home for nine days, and then I went to the hospital and was there till the symptoms were well dried.

When the doctor found out that I was able to come out he, Dr. Schenck, wrote to my lady to send a carriage out. She did so at once and I was at my mother's for awhile, and then my lady came to see me and told me how the woman did the people in the house, so I told her how bad my limbs were, and she said that if I could go home with her and tell her what to do, she would get on without the woman and let her go. My mother made me ready in a little while and I was soon at the dear old home, 344 Carlton avenue.

God be praised for the way he has led me since, I was three years old until this day, for it was His hand that taught me to remember all of these long years. I have in my mind the time at the old home when they put me on the fine dressing table in front of the large mirror, while the Rev. Mr. Walker baptized me in the name of the Father and the Son and the Holy Ghost, according to the Methodist tests in those days, and I always thought that was to give me my Christian name; but when the Lord had spoken peace to my soul He led me to follow in his footsteps, and I gladly followed Him to be buried to the world— that is, to be put out of sight, and that is what the word means. I have found it to be one of those times when the Father was pleased with His own dear beloved Son, and I know that He will be pleased whenever we do please Him, for God so loved the world of sinful men that He gave His only begotten Son that whosoever believeth in Him should have everlasting life, for God sent not His Son into the world to condemn it, but that through Him all might believe in Him and have everlasting life.

I wish that I could know that the whole world was receiving this life, and that we all could help to crown Him, as the angels are crowning Him, the King of Kings and Lord of Heaven and of this earth.

It is a blessed hope to know that God is love, and they that worship Him must worship Him in spirit and in truth.

I joined the church in 1866 and began to try and follow in this good old way that leads from earth to glory, and it has not always been a path of the sweetest flowers, but I have never failed to find my all in the Lord Jesus Christ.

He led me on day by day, and after a while I found that He had led me to go away from home that I might get ready for the work that my heart was so full of, for every time that I saw the newspaper there was some one of our race in the far South getting killed for trying to teach and I made up my mind that I would die to see my people taught. I was willing to go to prepare to die for my people, for I could not rest till my people were educated. Now they are in a fair way to be the people that God speaks of in the Holy Word, as He says that Ethiopia shall yet stretch forth her hand and all nations shall bow unto her. I long to see the day that the Ethiopians shall all bow unto God as the One that we should all bow unto, for it is to Him that we all owe our homage and to be very grateful to Him for our deliverance as a race. If we should fail to give him the honor due there would a curse come to us as a race, for we remember those of olden times were of the same descent of our people, and some of those that God honored most were of the Ethiopians, such as the Unica and Philop, and even Moses, the law-giver, was of the same seed.

And not long ago darkness hung over the face of this race and God moved upon the face of this dark earth and the light came forth.

How wonderfully solemn and yet grand are these inspired thoughts and words of a race whose God is so loving and forgiving, and we, contemplating the grand mystery of the world beyond this vale of tears, for God does preserve all that He has planted on this earth.

No subject can surely be a more delightful study than the history of a slave girl, and the many things that are linked to this life that man may search and research in the ages to come, and I do not think there ever can be found any that should fill the mind as this book.

This is a perfect representation of things as I can remember them, and to think how wonderful are these most beneficent streams of God's providence to all those of our race that have prayed that their loving children might feel the warm streams of an education flowing through every child. Tens of thousands of miles, North, South, West and East, God has thrown His mantle of love all around us, and it is that which should make us love and fear Him, who is able to destroy both soul and body; for His searching eye rests on all of the negro race, to see what use they are going to make of their time and talent, and I hope that nature will teach them that all of our talent belongs to the great God who gave us our being.

Nature awakens in our being a feeling that we must lay at His feet that we may get the blessed approval, for we are so changeable, but God is unchanging. He is omnipotent, and all else is transition. Yet God rules the oceans, the mountains, the valleys, and all that walks the broad earth.

Well, now I shall tell you something more of my working in the City of Brooklyn. I lived with the Bailley family the first year, and when they went away in the summer, as all of the rich used to do, I stayed in the house for the summer and they went across the ocean and were away for some time. The next year I did not like to stay in the house alone, so Mrs. Bailey got me a place with a nice friend of hers, and when she came home, thought that she was going to have me to come back to live with her but I stayed with her friend as there were but three in the family and the work was not hard, and it gave me more time to study, and Mrs. Stafford's son, Willie, was so glad to have me as his pupil that I had not any trouble to get my lessons ready for him. He went to school every day and he could not get through his head how it was that I could not go to school every day as he did. His mother told him how it was and his eyes would fill with tears and he would ask his mother and father to let him stay at home on Sundays to read the Bible to me while I should get the dinner ready, and they would let him stay, for he wanted to see me going to the House of God on Sundays as they did and was willing to have anything to eat that I might have the opportunity of attending the church and Sunday-school. His mother would let me go to the Sunday-school on every Sunday, for they were good people and were of the kind that delighted in their help and they were members of the Church of The Messiah, and they were a very happy family. They did not think that anything was too good for my enjoyment and that is the reason that I stayed with them and did not go back to the lady as she wanted me to do. I could not tell which seemed to love me most, and then her son was so willing to teach me, as Miss Abbie Bailley had, so I made up my mind that as I had more time there for study I would remain, and I had some of the best days of my life when I began to learn so fast, and he would bring me before his mother and father that they might hear me recite my lessons and see how well I was doing under him as my teacher. They felt the more glad to see how much he was interested in teaching me. Later on in years I was taken sick with the smallpox and was carried away to the hospital. He was taken sick while I was away and his mother said that he would call for me about the last one on this earth, and she tried to find me, but she did not know where I was for some time after his death, and then she felt so bad to think that he was gone and did not see me, for he always loved to be with me that he might hear me sing, as I was always on the wings of song if I were at my work; and that is the way that I have been all of my life.

When I got well of the smallpox, as I said, I went back to the place where I was living when I took the malady, and there I tried to work, but was very feeble for a long time and under the doctor's care all of the time and spending more than I could make, for some of the doctors charged me two dollars a visit, and that will use up a poor person's earnings very soon.

But all of this time I kept in mind the idea that I should save every cent that I could that I might send myself to school some day. That day did come when it seemed as dark as any night I had ever seen, when I should go away to boarding school and spend that little and should not have enough to finish; but I went, taking the Lord as the guide of my life, and the way began to grow bright before me and I could see all the clouds rolling away and the brightness shining forth. I went to Washington, D. C., and entered the Wayland Seminary, under the leadership of Professor G. M. P. King, of Bangor, Maine, with his other teachers and professors under him; all of whom are a noble band of teachers. And the way the Lord did help me in my studies is a blessing to the dear ones that I had under me for the eleven years that I was in the school work, and the way they progressed.

I said that I attended the Wayland Seminary for three years, of eight months, making it in all of my stay there twenty-four months, which may seem long to some, but it seems short to me, though I am very glad that I had that much time there for it was a fountain of blessing to my soul.

I left Washington, D. C., in the year of 1878 and came to Brooklyn and went to work again to earn money to go off to school, and when I did go it was another school in the Blue Ridge, Alleghany Mountains, where the very air of heaven seemed to fan the whole hill sides, and there never was a more lovely place on this earth for one to learn a lesson, for we could see the key to all lessons where nature had designed for a grand school of learning. At this place was to be found one of the best schools of learning that has been built by man. And I think of the hundreds and thousands of teachers and preachers and lawyers and doctors that these two schools have turned out in the different parts of this country, and many of them are in other parts of the world.

And all of this has been done through the churches, and God be praised for those that have given of their means.

At Harper's Ferry I spent four years and they were years of hard labor, but they were just as sweet as they could well be, for the Lord went with me and I found favor with all of the teachers. When I had spent the first eight months there I learned to have the greatest love for my beloved teachers, and when the time came for me to leave the teachers I thought that my poor heart would break. Though I was coming to my own people in Brooklyn, I felt that I was leaving my best friends on the earth and so did all of the students.

Well, now the Summer had passed and gone and the Fall came when God permitted all of the loving ones to come together once more to take up the cares of studies again. So the time of the winter season was always a blessing to all, and some found it the happiest time of their lives, for they found Jesus precious to their souls and could study so much better than they could before.

CHAPTER IV

There were sometimes as many as sixty or seventy brought to the knowledge of the Truth, and sometimes we had to go out of the class-room into the prayer-room, for the Lord was among us in the Spirit's power.

When in 1886 I went out for good, that I might be of some use to my own people I started in the strength of the Lord, and He did give me the greatest victory as a school teacher, for all of the people sought me to take their children in my school and give them a start. I had my hands full of work, but I let them come in for the Board always sent them to me find out if I could find room and time, and I always made the time for when scholars find that a teacher loves them they will do any amount of hard studying.

And so the time rolled on, with everything to make me feel like hard work, in the strength of the blessed Lord.

I was three years old when I was leaving my own dear mother's home to go to my new mother's home, or I should say to my white mother's home, to live with her, and I left my mother's as happy as any child could leave her own home, for this lovely lady was always at my mother's to see me ever since I could remember anything, and she was the joy of my little life and I seemed to be all the joy of her sweet life. She had learned to love me from the time that I came into the world.

She had watched me in my cradle and longed for the day to come when I should be able to walk, for she knew that I would follow her everywhere she should go. She said to all of the friends around that if I should live to remember her that would be all that she would ask.

And so she read her blessed Bible and prayed until she saw her prayers answered, and then she went to her home in glory, where she has watched and waited and longed to see the good old ships of those who have washed their robes and made them white in the Blood of the Lamb.

I can never tell any one how many happy hours that I had, for the only trial that I had was that of sickness, which caused me to be of a great care to her all of her life. It was her delight to wait on me and to have her cousin, the doctor, to be always ready to come at any moment she should send for him. He was a good doctor by the name of Sims, and I always liked him, too, until I had the typhoid fever and I had to take some oil. I did not like to take it and he held my hands so that they could pour that in me, and he and I fell out.

My white mother used to give it to me, but she did not let me know what she was giving me, for she put some molasses in the oil and cooked them, so I should not know. I would not have known if I had not seen her one night have the old bottle in her hand putting the oil in the kettle, which she was making ready for me, and I looked up and saw what it was and, as young ones will do, did not want to take molasses and butter which I had been taking so long, for I had to take it on every night or I could not speak.

Later on she moved from the place where she was and bought another farm where it was not near the water, as the doctor thought that was not a good place for me to be, and I was not sick so much as I had been at the former.

The first hard spell of sickness on this farm was the fever that I was sick of at the time that she took sick of the yellow jaundice, and she turned as yellow as anything could be. She went home with that awful malady, thinking of me and of what my future should be in God's hands, to love and bless the world in which I should live if it should be the will of Him who knows the future of all the people that live on this earth.

So God has been a father and a loving mother and all else to me, and sometimes there has been enough of trials in this life to make me almost forget that I had this strong arm to save me from these trials and temptations; but when I fly to Him I find all and in all in Him.

He is my rock and my hiding place in the time of trials, for a child that had all of the love and comfort of a queen was now left to her own dear mother, who had so many more and had to work so hard to take care of us all that I have seen sit up all night long working for her little ones. I used to feel sorry to see her sitting up alone at her work. I would get up out of the bed and sit with her till daylight; for I was always near mother after the dear one had been plucked from this earth to await my arrival.

I have found that learning is to refine and elevate the mind, so we should cultivate our hearts and minds and live to bless those we meet. We should neither flatter nor despise those that are rich or great.

It was not long after this dear one had been called away

before we were all in different places, and to share the fate that comes to those that are left behind those that have been good and kind. Then the time is coming that mother is to be taken from the whole family of little ones and they are to be left in the hands of others. That is one of the saddest times of life for children when they do not know if they shall ever see her face on this green earth any more; and if to-day we should hear the cries of those little lambs it surely would break the heart of a stone, for remember that we have the same feelings for our mothers as any race of people and our hearts will melt as easily as the richest ones on this earth.

But God in His great love to us meant that we should see the return of our dear mother to her own and that he would send her and the children out of the Land of Egypt as He did of old when He had tried to teach the rulers how wrong it was to sell and buy human flesh, and this was one of those awful sins that had to be repented of by those that could and would not see the truth. When the wrath of God came upon them and took all of the slaves away from them they could see nothing but tears and curses to the God of Heaven, and some of them cursed the earth, the stars, the moon. The negroes that had prayed so hard to God said that was the cause of the war, for they could see something in their prayers that seemed to reach up to heaven, and the answer had come for their deliverance.

Is not this a great God who can hear the prayers of the faithful ones when they pray? Do not we owe our lives and our all to this great and good God the Father, God the Son and God the Holy Ghost? And if we should fail to recognize Him we should have a worse sin fall on us than ever any one race had.

Well, to my story:

My brother James was my mother's oldest child. He was sent away to the war to keep his master at home, and we did not hear from him for a long time, but we made up our minds that if he did not get killed he would go over to the Northern side as soon as he should get the chance, though we did not see him to tell him to do so, for all of my mother's children were like herself in the love of freedom. My mother was one that the master could not do anything to make her feel like a slave and she would battle with them to the last that she would not recognize them as her lord and master and she was right.

My brother did try to get away, but he was caught and locked up in Richmond, Va., and for awhile we heard them say that he would be killed, but God was there to help him, so he came out all right and went to work on the breastworks, and when he did try again he got over on the Northern side. They almost caught him again, but as the Lord was his leader at night, he made his escape, and to hear him tell of that river that he crossed and how he walked on the water and he was so scared that he did not know he got wet; but I know that he did get wet, though. He said the Lord carried him over the river without letting him get wet. I am sure that I could not help laughing at my brother to hear of such a thing, for there never was a time that I have read of since the time of Peter that any one was called to walk on the water. The Lord was there Himself to show Peter how small his strength was when he trusted in his own strength, and Peter would have failed entirely if his Lord and Master had not been there.

And so it would have been with my dear brother. He would have been taken by the Southerners, and that would have been his last trial on this side of the grave.

My sister Frances was hired out and we did not see her from one Christmas to the other, for she was a good way off where she could not get home. She was treated very badly by some of those where she lived and her limbs had been sprained so that she could hardly move on them. When later on the Lord had it so arranged that she was taken home to live, where she could be cared for; she soon got better and was able to go about helping mother, with the rest of the children, for my brother who had to help her to care for the children was gone, and she was all the help that my mother had, for I was not large enough to do much and had not been put to mind the children.

The gentleman that my dear brother belonged to was a Methodist and a minister. He did not want to go to the war and so he sent my poor brother to defend what belonged to him, and he did not get the good of it after all, for my brother was determined that he would gain his freedom if he could and he tried and did not get tired of trying.

Then my sister Annie was given to the gentleman's married son and she was not with us, and sister Tempy Green was with the minister, and she was one of the dead ones that mother had a time to get. Maggie, Susie, Martha and Mary were at the same place where mother was sold from, and she went and got them at once. It was like a dream to them to see how far she had been sold and to see her back there again.

Sister Lavinia was at the same place where I was and she was treated very badly by the man's own daughter, for she would whip her without cause. Sister Rosa was at the same place and she was three and a half years on mother's return. As I told you, she was six weeks old when mother was sold and that made it three years and three months that mother was gone from her own native home to a part of the country where she did not know any one, not even the great God who had been so good to her all of those years when she was gone; and all of her whole life God was watching over her and giving to the world one child who was to help to educate the down-trodden race which was, through Abraham Lincoln, to be God's leader for the children that were in Egypt in the South, and God with this leader and the race, they came through fire and smoke, and now they can see the light of another day. Some of the race say that they are sometimes, in their thoughts, ashamed that they belong to a race that has been in bondage, but I have never felt that way, for I am glad that things have been as they were, for God has moved in a way that is unknown to men and His wonders He has performed, and has planted His footsteps in the South, the West, the East and in the North, and is watching the people and asking them what doors are they opening for the Ethiopian.

Father Abraham is calling to the Ethiopians to know what has been the result of the great emancipation, and can we not send the echo back with a jublilee, that we are marching on in education in double file, and longing to see the day that not one of your sons and daughters of this broad earth but what shall learn to read and write; though it may bless the earth with a tenfold blessing that they will not forget to bless God with a hundred fold.

Three cheers for this great Emancipator.

And while he may sleep yonder, forgotten may be by some,

his name has a green spot in my heart and shall ever keep green while on this side I stay.

And there is another one who sleeps yonder whom I shall not forget and that is Father John Brown, whose ashes are as dear to me as the apple of mine eye; and how can I forget him after four years of study at the dear old place where he was taken from and hanged, because he saw the wrath of God upon the nation and came forth to save his people.

Another one who will ever be shining bright in the hearts and minds of the whole negro race, and what shall I say of him who led us to the greatest victory the world has ever known—Ulysses S. Grant, the loved of all nations and the pride of all lands; he whom the world admires, to call the blessed, who mourned for this land to see the end, and God did help him in ways that man knew not, save himself and his God.

And there is another dear one that God will help me to remember with all of the love and gratitude, and it makes me feel sad as I have to speak of her once more and it may be that I shall have to speak of her many times, as she was the one that brought me on to this lovely city, and that is my mother, who has gone to that land of song where there is no more of sickness or sorrow and where God will dry every tear.

There is another I remember and that is Father Charles Sumner, who for years wrote and also fought and spoke, as never man spoke, for the race and the Civil Rights Bill, that it might not die, but it should be a rock for the defence of the race.

And there is another that I shall not leave out of this book, for if I did the book would be incomplete, and that is Frederick Douglass, the greatest of men among the negro race of this country or of any land on the globe. He wrote and spoke and went all over to try to do all he could for his race, and who could forget such men as these? I would say in true lines, may the earth fail to move sooner than I forget those noble-lives. Honored be their memories and honored be their ashes, for their lives shall live in the memories of all coming generations and their ashes will make rich the soil whereon they lie.

May God give us some more of such men as these for they are few, and we need so many now to go forth and speak the truth.

And there is dear Doctor David Moore, that my pen, I fear, would fail to move, if I did not do him honor. He was beloved and honored to the last day of his stay in the Washington Avenue Baptist Church, and it was on account of sickness that he had to leave this city and go up in the northern part of this State that he might be able to preach the Word, and God did make him well after he had left Brooklyn; and his work has been crowned with great success.

God did use him in this city to His own glory in saving men, women and children from the very door of sin and the dread of the life which is to come. And may the God of Heaven and the Ruler of this earth be with him as he comes near the Jordan to make its waters calm, and enter in the gate and hear the blessed "Well done, good and faithful servant, enter thou in the joys of thy Lord."

J. D. Fulton is one that will have one of the highest places at God's right hand, for he started out to look after the Ethiopian's rights when he was only seventeen years of age. What can be said of a long life like his, that has written and traveled and spoke to such large crowds of hearers in the interest of the race which I represent. How I have seen those silvery locks fly as his warm heart melted to tears as he pleaded for the down-trodden of the Ethiopians; and if God has ever heard a prayer I know that He hears the prayer of this dear good man, for I have seen the answer come in mighty power, in many ways, to the saving of precious souls, and the way that he wrote about the negro in this country and its problem.

He was called to the Hanson Place Church to preach and he worked hard, with God's help, and improved the church and many were brought to the Saviour through the Word, such as the Lord will own and bless at the last day.

Doctor Fulton is one of the best men on this broad earth to love and labor for humanity and I do not think that my race, the noble Ethiopians, should ever forget him as long as God shall spare his life. When the time shall come when the dear blessed one shall be called to the world above, and that active form is stilled in death and when that silvery voice is no longer heard in the defence of the down-trodden Ethiopians and the oppressed of any land, that he will hear the "Well done, good and faithful servant, enter thou into the joy of thy Lord."

And to think of one who has written so long never more to wield the pen in the cause of the church and God's children is a sad thought to the writer, for she has loved him as a father and he shall ever have a green spot in my heart for I shall never forget his kind words to me in my lonely hours.

Dr. J. D. Fulton's first wife was one of the loveliest women that ever lived, for I have been to their house to dine with the family and I found that Mrs. Sarah Fulton and family were the same that they were in the church. There was the sweetest home that I ever saw in all my life, for the father and the mother were all love, and then take Miss Jennie, the eldest child, and she was a lovely girl, and there was Miss Nellie, another lovely girl, and Sadie, the youngest girl, and she was her father all the way, and the boy Justin, who came to the family while I was away. I think he has a large heart like his dear father, and I do know that if he only is a good man like his father God will own and bless him.

Dr. Fulton's second wife, Aunt Laura, was a lovely woman, for we all learned to love her when her first husband was living.

Miss L. A. Pousland was one of the best ladies I have seen in this city, for it was from her house that I went to the Wayland Seminary in 1875, and to her love I owe a love of gratitude, and to all that may come to me as worldly goods I shall always think of Miss L. A. Pousland and of her love to me when I was getting ready for school and the letters full of love to me all the time while I was prosecuting my studies. Oh, how she longed to see me out in the world doing my Master's will and helping to teach, for she is a Boston lady, and they are a learned people and like to see all others learn, and that is the way, like the old Pilgrim Fathers were, that there should be a grand common level for all after them.

To my story of child in House's family:

This Mr. John House had the largest sum offered to him for a girl as I was that was ever offered for any one and he would not accept the whole world of money, on account of the one that had loved me and cared for me, for he well knew that after all of those prayers that he would be sinning; and he would not have had my mother sold away from her children if his brother would have let him know it in time. He went away to attend court and to his surprise found that my mother was sold. He came home at once to let us know of it, and he was the one that called in my sister Frances and sister Annie and sister Rosa, for the two oldest that I speak of fell to a dead brother who had drank himself to death, and these were sold to pay for his drink. He had been dead for some time and those that he owed now came in to get their pay, which was their only chance; and the money that they got did not do them much good, thanks to God, for it was in the time of the war and the money was of the Confederate money, and it was during the great struggle when this money was called in never more to be the money of these United States, for this Union needs the kind of money that will be good in all lands, and I am glad that the people can see it now as they never saw it before.

CHAPTER V

I am glad that the dear Lord has laid it in my heart at this time in life to let the world hear something of a life that they will all be filled with a love for one whom it has been a delight to meet at any and all times.

Mrs. Sarah Potter, who is a beloved and dear lady, who is the bright morning star of the Washington Avenue Baptist Church, and who is one of the brightest lights that this city has or ever will have, for she is all over this city looking after the needy ones, comes from a noble family and all of the family have been foreign missionaries. She has been a home missionary for many years and God has blessed her and her labors, and her dear father was doing missionary work in India for fifty years, and God blessed his work there. Now that his dear work has been finished in this world and he has gone to his reward, his works do follow him, for the number that have been saved through his preaching eternity will tell.

His form will no more walk out on the field of battle for the

Lord, and who can fill the place of such a life-work as this child of the King has filled? And to go home to his beloved and blessed Master with his arms full of blessed sheaves; and as we think of him, how we wonder in our daily walks if we shall go to the Saviour with our hands full or shall we go empty-handed and thus to meet our Saviour so; not one soul with which to greet Him, must we empty-handed go?

I have heard of Mr. Mason as one of the first to go among the Coreans, and I have seen some of them, that have taken the Lord for their all and in all, come to this land of ours to fit themselves for the blessed work among their own people. God be praised for such a man as Dr. Mason and all of his loving children, who have had the same spirit that their father had, and he was filled with the Holy Ghost and with the power of the Lord.

Mrs. Sarah W. Potter was the beloved wife of a sea captain, Mr. William Potter, and he owned a ship that sailed the Indian Ocean, and he was washed overboard one night while his wife, Mrs. Potter, was sick, and she did not know that he had a watery grave until the next day. They had one son, who is now married, by the name of Frank, whom I held as an idol, as he always called to me when in trouble, for his dear mother taught him the love of the Bible, and he would not fight any boy, let them do him as they would. He knew that I would go after the boys for blocks, as I was one of those soldiers that was not afraid to fight. As he grew older I told him that he had to go out into the world to fight his way and I wanted him to begin it at once, and he did learn to battle for himself. He married a lovely girl by the name of Miss Katie Harvey and they have two children, the eldest a girl and the youngest a boy, which is the lovely little man of the home.

I have seen that mother sit up at nights waiting for her son to come that she might ask a blessing on him before he should sleep, and how could that boy go astray after all these prayers and entreaties? May he lead his lambs to the blessed Master, and have the "Well done, good and faithful servant, enter thou into the joys of thy Lord."

To my story of work in the City of Brooklyn:

The lady, Miss L. A. Pousland, whom I spoke of in the preceding pages, is the place where I found myself living in 1875, after twelve or thirteen years of service. It was there that I met Mrs. Sarah Potter. She has been all of a mother to me to give me all the encouragement she could bestow on me. For all of this kindness I am more than grateful to my Heavenly Father, for I know that all goodness comes from Him. He surely has shown His love to her in sparing her to see me go from her home to Washington to school and spend three years and then go to Harper's Ferry and spend four years, and to see me out in the world teaching for eleven years, and to break down while at my post and now at home to serve in another way. Is not this not God's love to me, as a poor, humble servant of His? I should never forget to give the love and honor due Him.

God knows my heart and He will bless the work in my hands, as the writer of this book.

When I found that I could get through school in a given time as I had studied hard, if I had the money, I told Miss L. A. Pousland, that I would not be there to work any more, as I had a place in Saratoga Springs for the Summer. She felt bad to lose me, but as she knew that I could make more money for three months at the Springs she wanted me to have my heart's desire, so I came on from school and went to see her and then made ready for the Springs, getting one of my sisters to go with me and taking such things as we could. We were there too soon and we had to wait for work, and I went around and made myself known to the white people. They soon called on me to come and do work for them, and the first was a Mrs. Carpenter, a good lady. She then got her married daughter to have me to work for her family and they were a fine family. Her daughter's husband was a grand studio man on Broadway, doing a good business. Then she sent me to another friend of hers, and my sister and I could live for a while. When the rush came I did not forget the one who had helped me, but went to her two days out of a week, for she had her house filled with boarders, and the Summer was all a blessing to her and her family.

There was Mrs. Purdy, who was another one of my friends, for I did work for her laundry for three years, and she said whenever I came to the Springs and wanted work to come to her; if the house was filled there was room for me. So you see how God did open the way for me in that strange and lonely place, where there are so many that go there for the Summer looking for work. I went out of the house where we were stopping and got the washing and brought it home to my sister, for she would not go out of the house as she had not been from the place where she lived before. I got her to go with me to help me with the work, and it was coming in so fast I had to get a white lady to help us to get through, for the colored people said that we would not get work as the laws were passed to keep the New York workers out, and I told them that they would have to pass laws to keep the rich people of New York from coming there to board if they should keep the workers out; so I did not hear to that, and found the way for I had the will, and where there is a will there is always a way. So much for the first Summer.

Well, the second time I went up alone. I say alone, I mean that my sister did not go, but the Lord did go with me that Summer, for I did not go to the house where my sister and I was for they tried to discourage us the first time. I always mark one that is an enemy to me and shake the dust off of my feet and let the Lord do for that one what He thinks is best.

Well, for the third year I was there with the Lord and He was surely there with me. I did not do any work on the Lord's Day, but tried to teach them. When they made me an offer of larger pay for the work done on the Lord's Day, I told them that in six days the Lord made the heavens and the earth and He rested on the seventh day, and I felt that if He needed rest on that day I was sure that I must have rest. So the Sunday work was not carried on any more in that laundry. He said that the Lord had sent me to that laundry for the bettering of all in it. The gentleman was from Philadelphia and his name was Mr. Cheek.

So you see how the Lord preached His word through me, a feeble one of the dust, and what can not the Lord help us to do if we only trust in Him and if we strive to live for His honor and glory while on this side of Jordan?

Mrs. Purdy had one daughter, and a lovely girl in music, and her name was Kittie Purdy. She was sought to play everywhere as she was a fine player, and everyone thinks her a very pretty girl. Her mother is a perfect lady, for she used to be so kind to her help. She never was late in any of her meals for the help and she always sat down with us and eat with us. She was as jolly as any one at the table and she always called me her bird, for I was on the wing of song from the time I began my work until my work was finished, and then I would start home as happy as any one could be. Then I would be the first to greet her in the mornings always and she used to say that I brought to her a great deal of comfort each hour and drove all of her business cares away. I used to feel glad that I, although a working girl, could be of some love and comfort to some one, and it makes me feel glad to-day that God in His love to me and for me can own such a feeble one.

My next start was for Asbury Park to do work for Mrs. Haseltine, another lovely lady, who was a Boston lady and whom I learned to love as a mother. I worked for her two years and was to have worked for her the third year if she had not taken sick at the time she did. A gentleman came on from Philadelphia and she got me to work for him and I found him a fine gentleman. I praise God for all that came to me while I was pursuing my studies, and to-day I do feel like saying,

> "Blessed assurance, Jesus is mine,
> Oh! what a foretaste of glory divine;
> Heir of salvation, purchase of God,
> Born of His spirit, washed in His blood.
> This is my story, this is my song,
> Praising my Saviour all the day long,
> This is my story, this is my song,
> Praising my Saviour all the day long."

To my story: Mrs. Haseltine, I said, had to go to the Saratoga Springs for the Summer and she used to let me hear from her, but my work in school was so great that I lost sight of her and I do not know if she is in Florida or not. Wherever she is I love her and she has my heart. She did all that she could all the time that I worked for her to let me do extra work for the boarders so that I might earn money outside of what she paid me, and the

ladies used to come to the laundry and talk to me, for some of
these ladies went to school as I did and some of them waited at
the large hotels in the Summer time to pay their board. The
gentleman that had Mrs. Haseltine's house took me in at
evening time to entertain the guests, and they all helped me.
When I came home to make ready for school I was at our own
church one evening when dear Dr. J. D. Fulton was giving us
one of his grand lectures, and he gave me time to sing, read and
speak. The church took a grand collection for me, which
amounted to seventeen dollars and seventy-three cents. I was
better fixed that year than I had been at any year since I had
been going to school, for I had worked all of the Summer and
would not spend any of my money as I wanted it all for school,
but the Evil one came and stole it from me and I was left without a dollar, and I had the heavy heart one is sure to have when
they need money as I did. Then I had to borrow money to leave
for the school, and you may think how one feels after a
Summer's work, and to have some one else to use the money
that has not been gotten with their own labor.

Well, I did not know what I should do, so I made up my mind
that I had done all that lay in my power—that is, I had earned
the money, and some one had taken it from me and I was left to
go without. So I took the Lord for it, and could not board as I
had done, but I bought some little things to use and boarded
myself, and I was up sometimes at the late hours of night, when
all of the people were asleep, cooking for the next day, that I
might not be late at school. So you can see how loving God was
to me.

My life in school was one of joy to me and to my mother and
sisters and brother and brothers-in-law, and all of the time that
I was in school they were sending me their mites to help me
along. My sister, Mrs. E. F. Rodwell and Mr. G. W. Rodwell,
and my sister, Mrs. Annie Lindsey and Mr. F. P. Lindsey, were
the ones that never for once forgot me, and at Christmas time
I was like a child looking for something. Everybody was good to
me. Praise the Lord for all of the love that came to me in the
time of need.

Well, my work ended in 1886, though I taught in 1885, and

had the blessing of God with me in this school. There were twenty-five out of the school brought to the knowledge of the truth, such as the Lord will own and bless at the last day. God be the glory. Amen and Amen.

The place was Woodstock, Shenandoah County, Va., and I was called from that school to go West where they needed me to teach in a place where the teachers had made the pupils almost hate to go to a school. My heart was in that work, which no one liked, so I went there trusting in the Lord. I lost that place, but they got me another one where they built me a new house, and the Lord did bless me in this place, although I was not able to go to the Baptist Church only once a month, for there was not any nearer than ten or fourteen miles. When the next year came I helped the people build a church and it was all paid for before I left there. How God did pour out His spirit there in the salvation of souls, and He did add unto the dear church such as will be saved at the day when He shall come to make up his jewels; and I can praise His name for such a Saviour.

Well, to my story: As a teacher in the same place for eleven years, or I should say I was connected with the same school for that length of time, and all the way the Saviour led me. Sometimes it was not all flowers and sweetness, but in it all I can see the hand of the Blessed One, and it used to make me say to myself, Praise the Lord, Oh, my soul, and all that is within me praise His holy name!

After being there for sometime I was taken sick and was there sick and could not teach my school for that Winter. It made me feel very bad, but my good Dr. Ford said that he thought all of the county were sorry to learn of my illness and all were losing a good teacher. I would not be able to do any school work for sometime to come as the nerves were all overworked, and that had brought on other troubles which were of a dangerous nature. So my heart was heavy indeed, and if I had not had my hope built in Jesus Christ I would not have stood, for I felt that all other ground was to me a sinking sand. I stayed there all of the Winter and then came on home to Brooklyn, and the Lord was so good to make me well; I went back to my work and taught all that Winter, and when my school was out I then went down to the county seat, which is ten miles from the station and is about fourteen from my school, where I spoke of.

Hinton is a lovely little town on the Chesapeake and Ohio Railroad and in the Blue Ridge and Alleghany Mountains, and is one of the greatest places on the road, as all of the trains from the West, East, South and North stop there. It is a lovely town and they have a roundhouse there where they build locomotives. They have a fine Y. M. C. there. There are a number of men employed at this place. They have two nice Baptist Churches and a Baptist Mission, two Methodist Churches, one Episcopalian, one Congregational, one Presbyterian and one Roman Catholic and one college, a number of private schools and a number of public schools and the county is doing a good work in education, and to the Lord be all the praise for all of this good work.

Hinton I said was a lovely place. Like Harper's Ferry, that I spoke of in the preceding chapter, it is situated on Camp Hill in a lovely place, between the Potomac River on one side and the Shenandoah River on the other, and it has two of the most beautiful bridges I ever saw. When you see the trains coming and going it looks lovely.

The Wayland Seminary is in a lovely spot on Meredian Hill, between Fifteenth and Sixteenth streets, and you can see all over the City of Washington. It is lovely to behold with all of its fine buildings and art galleries, though I do not like it as well as Harper's Ferry, for I was not well the whole time I was there and I had so much better health at the Ferry. I bless God that I made the change when I did or I might have been gone to my long home before I had the time to see so much of God's love to me in the way He has led me through paths that I did not see then. I can truly say unto Him, Lord, Thou hast been my dwelling place in all of these years of trial and has been my rock in a weary land and my shelter in the times of storm.

Well, I came home last October a year ago, 1895, and made up my mind to stay for the time being. Some of the people found out that I was here and they sent for me to come to see them. I went to Mrs. Murphy's the next week and I was there nearly a year and found that I could not do much lifting, so I did not feel well for quite a while, and I had a heavy day of it the last time that I was there. So I told her daughter I should not come any more as I had gone early that I should get home early. It was nealy six o'clock when I stopped. They are a lovely family of four men and four girls, all of whom are very fine indeed; two sons married, and children, and one daughter married and she has two little ones. Miss Josephine is a school teacher, Miss Alice is the housekeeper, as the mother is not very well at times. One of the lovely girls is a Sister in a convent.

I also did work for her daughter, Mrs. Nellie Chester, and she is a lovely woman. I had to lose her work as she had to get her a girl.

I also worked for fine families by the names of Mrs. Handford and Mrs. Taylor, but they went away from this city.

CHAPTER VI

I am now doing work for a lovely family by the name of Mrs. Coddington, as her husband has died not long since, and he was a nice man and they have two lovely girls that teach school. I also work for Mrs. White, who is a lovely lady, and all of her family.

At the Pells and the Powells. Mrs. Pell is a lovely woman, with two children, one a lovely young lady and full of the sweetest music the ear ever heard, for I do not think that there ever was any one that could play sweeter music than her. The other is a boy, a nice youngster of promise.

Mrs. Powell is the sister of the first Mrs. Pell and she has one daughter, who is a Mrs. Pell, whom I have to call Mrs. E. Pell to let each one know which one I mean. There are other ladies in the mansion that are very nice to me. Mrs. Pell No. 1 is the head of the house and is a fine lady, and in telling you of those that I have worked for and I am doing work for I mean to tell that it is by the day that I work for some of them; as you will see as you read this that I have had very few places where I lived out by the month, and staying a good while in a place.

I did work for Mrs. Johnson, but as her business is not so good at times she has me whenever she can feel as if she can spare the money. So this little life of mine has been almost locked up in a nutshell, and Jesus has come to me in the spirit's power that I should tell the world of His wonderful love to me a poor sinner of the dust. And what can not the Lord do for those who put their trust in Him? We feel like saying to the blessed One, how amiable are all of Thy works, oh Lord, and our eyes are seeing Thy salvation in many parts of the earth.

I can remember the first time that it was my pleasure to hear dear Dr. J. D. Fulton. It was on Thanksgiving Day when he first came to this city to preach at the Hanson Place Church, as their pastor. The Rev. David Moore had him to preach the Thanksgiving sermon at the Washington Avenue Baptist Church, and we were all delighted at hearing him on that day. I loved him on hearing that sermon, for I felt the spirit power on that day, through his preaching. I shall always think of the Doctor and his loving family, for we, as the negro race, have not such a friend on earth as Dr. Fulton. I am not afraid to say it to his dear honor as he is not dead, and I wish every negro knew him as I do for then they would all feel toward him as I feel. I hope that he will long live to tell the truth as he has in days gone by; and if he was in this city where the evil is so strong, we should hear him sounding the watchword, and that is the reason that those that loved the ways of sin did not like him, for they felt that he had cause to trouble them while they were yet in their sins.

But I hope that the day will come when I shall hear him again in this city, and I hope that God will give him long life and that he may see the travel of his soul and be satisfied, for I know that he tries to do God's will in this love that he has for humanity and that is why the Lord will bless him in all the work that his hands find to do.

I was not at home when he left this city and I felt sad when I found that he was gone, for we shall ever miss him. My prayer is to God that he may live to a good old age and that when he shall be called to come up higher that he may be caught up in the air to meet his Lord and Master and all of those that have gone on before, and be ready to Crown Him King of Kings and Lord of Lords.

Progress of Church Work

A speech to a crowded church, in the year of our Lord 1888, in Talcott, Summers Co., W. V. I was asked to have this published out there, but I wanted to have it brought to my home in Brooklyn. I was into so much work out there, and my people were not there to see what the Lord did help me to do:

Dear friends, we are here to-night to commemorate this grand occasion, and our watchword is Onward and Upward to the Prize!

This is a time that we should all shout the Jubilee and to send the glad tidings to all the world and to let all the nations know that we are on our march to that happy land of song.

Dear friends, let us look for a few moments and think of the time when you had not a church where you could worship God. I told you that God would give you this lovely place, where no one could drive you out, and to see what great things He has done for you in a little time, and how great things can He not do if we will only trust Him? We have those of our race that have held places of greatest trust and God bless them in those places. Why should we give up the fight and lay our armor by when there is so much for us to do? No, no, we can not and we will not lay the grand old armor down, for the Lord is on our side and we shall surely conquer if we look to Him whose arm is so large and strong. Then let us take fresh courage and march on until we reach the goal, and then we shall be glad and rejoice for the Lord has spoken good to His people, the Ethiopians.

Oh, ye colored people, why not take this as yours and begin now to rejoice ye in your own race and feel proud of the race, but not ones that can dance the best on the ballroom floor, for there is very little in that when it is all summed up in a whole. Let us thank all the good people who have shown any love to us while we have been in this work of building and may they all find favor in the sight of God. You have a dear good pastor who is willing to give his life to the Lord and the church. Let us take fresh courage and march into His service, for we shall gain if we only trust in God and do the right He will help us to persevere.

Time would fail me and my pen would fail to move if I should try to enumerate all of the blessings that have come to us as a race. I hope that we, as the hated negro race, will make a fresh start from this night and do all that we can to forward the work in this church, and God will send us a blessing.

Etiquette of Men

I was wondering a few days since if the men of the present day had lost the respect that men used to have for the women. I was carried back to the year of 1884 while in school with so many of the young men of my own race, when I saw so much of the respect that they showed to us girls and that was what caused me to write this to their honor. I think that true etiquette is one of the greatest blessings that young men can have for the women, for it is to them that we look to for the protection and love, and if we fail to find it in them where shall we look? This is one of the greatest fortunes that one can have, and it is that which makes a young man what he ought to be. We, as the women, need so many of such ones and the world needs them fully as much, and the God who made them looks for more and when he does not find it in the dear creatures that He has made it makes Him feel sad.

I found a number of young men that used to attend the Wayland Seminary that had the greatest regard for the girls, and I could not but notice them in this respect and their kind acts while there, although I was not in the same classes with them, but I never saw them make any difference while I was in school. I always found good friends among them and I never saw a young man meet one of the young ladies but they lifted their hats, and that made the people of Washington, D. C., always speak of it in the kindest terms. One never loses anything in this way, and their virtues are greater than gold.

When the weather was very bad one day and I was coming from school and a young man saw me fall down, he came to help me home and I felt very grateful, and I feel that wherever that young man shall go he will have favor in the eyes of all, and God will be his leader for he has made a good beginning.

School Life

While at the Harper's Ferry school I found the loveliest teachers that ever were in a school. Professor Brackett, the head of the school, is a fine gentleman, and his wife, Mrs. W. Brackett, is a lovely lady and she is one of the finest teachers that ever lived. She has three nice children, two of them are girls and one boy, who is a young man by this time, for I have not seen him since he went to Maine to attend school, which is the Bates'. It is a fine school of Latin, and a number of the students went to that same school.

Mr. W. P. Curtis was one of the professors. He was my Sunday-school teacher and he was fine.

Mr. D. M. Wilson was a dear professor, whom we loved. Miss Caroline Franklin was a lovely teacher and we all loved her. Miss C. Brackett was one of the lovely teachers, and one whom every one of the other teachers loved, for she was one of the finest readers that ever lived, let it be man or woman. They used to have her read nearly every afternoon when the school was out, and sometimes they would call to Professor Curtis to read to the school. He was a very good reader, but Miss C. L. Franklin was the grand trainer of the whole school. They had a grand reading circle there at nights for the rich of the Ferry, and she was the one to do the fine reading. All of the noble people of the place loved her and she will ever be loved and remembered by all who knew her. She is now in Washington, D. C., teaching, and the people have learned to love her as we did. I do not think that any one could help loving her for her love and fidelity to the race which she represents.

Miss C. L. Franklin's mother, who is a lovely woman whom we all love as a mother, for she had many of the students at her house to board, like Mrs. William Lovett, and she was so very kind to all of them that she will be remembered by us all, for we love those in our school life that would say a kind word to us. It was to help us along in our daily toil.

Mrs. Julia Robinson was one of the lovely ladies at the Ferry, also, and all of the teachers boarded there. She has a number of the students that board with her and she is much beloved.

Mrs. Bell was one of the ladies that kept boarders and she is much beloved. Mr. W. M. Bell is one of the teachers and all love him as a teacher.

Mr. J. Trinkle, who keeps one of the halls in the Summer time has a number of boarders, and does well all of the Summer months and in the Winter he teaches in or near the Ferry. With it all they are all doing what they can to help to forward the interest or an education in all of that section, and I really think that part of the country will show a larger percentage of those that have been educated through the churches than could have been taught in the public schools, for the terms are so very short that it is hard for the people to get a start.

But God has wonderfully blessed the teachers that have been sent on there from the North to look after the interests of the negroes. They love the work of the school-room, and it is their meat and their drink daily to give away what they have received. The Word says that it is more blessed to give than to receive, and we are always ready to receive from the hands of our earthly friends, and it is much greater to receive from God.

Mr. Thomas Lovett has two lovely little girls, named, respectively, Florence, the eldest, and the other Shoelett, and they are very smart. Mr. Lovett has built a hill-top house in a lovely place. It is filled in the Summer time, while he has music for the boarders. That makes it pleasant during the warm weather of the Summer months, and it is one of the loveliest places that can be found on the B. & O. Railroad, and the white people go there from all parts.

I had the pleasure of stopping there on my way home in 1895, and it did my soul good to find such a fine house built by one of the colored gentlemen and one that I had known, for I was at his mother's boarding house for the whole time that I was at the Ferry. He was teaching school then in the Winter time and looking after his mother's business in the Summer time. So I am glad that some of my people are trying to make an honest living. He is one among the many at the Ferry that are keeping boarding houses; and I am thankful for all that comes to us as a race. I hope, as I have often heard dear Dr. Fulton say that he wanted to see the race go forward, and I pray that the time is not far distant when all of the friends of the negroes shall see them making men and women of themselves, and then the grand problem will be solved. Then we shall be glad, for I am grieved night and day for my own people, and I feel so grateful to God for letting me see and to know that I have such a good friend as Dr. Fulton is. He shall be loved by me as long as I live, and I hope that he will ever be loved by all that shall read this life of mine, for he has been a father to me and I am one that always remembers a kindness as long as any one will do one for me. God will bless those that will think of me in love.

As this day has been one of quiet to me I have wondered what it would be to me if I could look into those bright mansions above and see my two mother's faces. What a joy there would be at the sight of them seeing me and of me seeing them, and we all singing,

Holy, holy, holy, Lord God Almighty.
  Early in the morning our songs shall rise to Thee;
Holy, holy, merciful and mighty,
  Casting down their golden crowns around the glassy sea.

And what a glory it will be for all that have washed their robes and made them white in the blood of the Lamb; and I know that two darling mothers have washed their robes and made them white, and to God be all the praise for the great love that He has shown to poor me, who feels so lonely on this lovely Lord's day. How much have I found in His service, too, and if I could be able to go there to-night I feel that I should be blessed, but I have to stay at home to-night as I have not been well for a month or more. I feel grateful as can be that I could be out this morning, and I will pay vows unto my God as long as I shall live, for He is my rock and my hiding place in the time of trouble. I have had a storm of them and it is to Him I fly to shield my soul from the evil one, and knowing as do how many hard spells I have had, it is right for me to be as careful as I can, taking the Lord for my healer. How He has blessed me so many times when there were no other hopes for me to build on, I have found that I could trust in His almighty power.

I shall not forget the kind care of Dr. Matthews, of this lovely city, whom God gave to me when I was very low and the three times a day that he paid his visits to see how I was getting along. He was so kind in his words to comfort me and to give my mother cheer I shall always think of him kindly, for the snow was so deep that a horse could not travel very well and he had to walk it three times a day. I had not my white mother then to care for me, but my own mother did what she could for me and I know that she has her reward in heaven for all that she has ever done for me in the times when I needed the most care.

There is good Dr. Reeves, a good Quaker doctor, and I had to have him to attend me. He was very kind and gentle in his treatment of me and I am very glad that I found such a friend in him, for he was like a father to me? I shall not overlook dear Dr. Warmsley, who was a good doctor to me and he was kind as he could be, and I shall not forget him, although I have not seen him for a long time.

What shall I say of the last doctor that I was under out West, and that is Dr. J. W. Ford, who was so kind to me as a stranger. He would come when he was sent for. It made no difference what time of day or night. It might be you would find him on his way where he was sent for and sometimes he would be on the road all night long, for he is the best doctor in the county, and I was going to say the best in the State of West Virginia. They all send for him; far and near, where they have any fever, and he is so good in fevers, through the Lord, he is sure to bring them out of if they do as he tells them. May the Lord give him a good long life to do the will of Him who is the greatest doctor after all. And if we only put our trust in Him we shall find that He will make our sick bed easy for us and He will carry us all the way while we are sick, for He has borne our sorrows and sickness.

To my story as a school girl: It was full of sweet love and regard, for I gained favor with all of the teachers and professors and all of the pupils. The Lord be praised for all of this love and joy that came to me in my school days. Then the love that came from the Washington Avenue Baptist Church of sending me the sum of twenty or thirty dollars to help me in paying my expenses was of the greatest love for one in a school, as I wanted to pay as I went, and then the Sunday-school would send me their money, one of the dear, loving favors of God's love, and naming each time from which the money came and sending it through the Board at Chicago. Then Mrs. Conley or Mrs. Connell sent it to me and the Board sent the same way when my own beloved church sent me money. It was in the time of Mrs. Sarah Fulton and she did not forget me when I was in school. The Mission Band of our church sent me some money every year after the first year that I went to school. Sometimes it was to the answer of my prayers that the money came at the time I needed it to pay my board and God be praised for those who from the bottom of their hearts contributed in the grand and good work of education. For all that I shall do in this life to help some one that needs help, I shall think of the Lord's love to me and try and do what I can to bring them to the Lamb of God that taketh away the sins of the world, and to God I owe my life and my all, and if I should fail to love and honor Him I know that He will not remember me before His dear Father in heaven.

Mr. William Lovett, the father of a large family, is one of the finest gentlemen anywhere around the whole country, and is much beloved by all who know him. The white people who board with him in the Summer time all liked him, for he was so nice and quiet. He has a large family of girls and boys and all are smart. He sent two of them to the Hillsdale College when they had finished at the Ferry, and one was John Lovett, who studied law, and the other one, Miss Etta Lovett, was a fine school teacher and a music teacher.

I have just learned that the last one of the girls has married, and that is the youngest of the family. They all have good partners for life, which does not come to all large families. God bless such a father and mother, who have taken such good care of the training of their children.

Mr. John Lovett was one of the teachers of whom I shall speak of, as I boarded in their house for four years. A more lovely woman never lived than his mother. She is known far and wide as one of the best ladies to keep boarders and she has a lovely family of girls and boys. Mr. Thomas Lovett is a school teacher and much beloved. He married a doctress, who is one of the finest ladies that lives, She is from the North and she has some of the best people of the Northern cities that she waited on, and they love her to-day for the kind care that she had for them.

Miss Emma Carter is one of the teachers, and Miss Lizzie Sims, Miss Frances Sims, Mr. Burrell and Mr. C. H. Plummer; and of later years Miss Mary Brackett has gone there as one of its teachers and there are others that have gone there as teachers. The dear good work is going on in the strength of the Lord and I hope that He will still bless his work. The same that I said of Miss C. L. Franklin I will say of Miss Lulia Brackett, who is married now and is still one of its beloved teachers. She loves the work of teaching the negroes better than her own life and all that she has in Maine. God bless those dear teachers, as they labor there for my own dear people whom God has blessed in getting an education.

Miss Lulia Brackett married a Mr. Loughtner, who is a schoolmaster for the whites at the Ferry, and who is a fine school teacher and whom the people like very much. It is a joy to meet him on his way to his school-house.

Mr. William Bell is one of the teachers whom we all love dearly, and he taught school outside for a while before he came to teach at the college. He had the greatest success as a teacher. May God bless those faithful ones as they are far from their homes, family, friends and loving ones.

I had the pleasure of working for a fine family in Brooklyn by the name of Davis, and I found them all a lovely family. I had the pleasure of going away in the country one Summer to a place called Flemington, N. J., and we had a fine time as it was his father and mother's home, and they had a dairy farm and all of the nice things that one finds in the country. I was not well while there as it was low land, and one of their daughters was not well, so I feeling that I would be better to come home they got ready and come on home, and I left them and went to my home where I could rest. In the Fall I was so much better that I was able to go back out West and take up my work again.

When I had finished my public school I taught a pay school for the Summer and had a large number of scholars, and they progressed well. Some of them would go without their food all day to study extra lessons.

It would be all of a joy to the whole world to have seen how well all of the girls, boys, young men and young ladies did in all of the schools where I have had the pleasure of teaching.

I have never taught in any school with any other teacher or teachers, and I was so much more blessed, for all teachers have a way of their own. The new teacher always makes so much change in a school and in the pupils, I found that to do good work in school I should stay long in one place, that I might bring the scholar near to me. Sometimes I have had it rough, but in it all I can see the hand of God leading me to do all that I could to help forward the great cause of education in those parts where there was so much need.

I have just learned that the Rev. J. D. Fulton has had a stroke and I cannot tell how he is at this time, but I can not do any work until I hear from him, as I have had my mind on him for some time, as he was somewhere in Massachusetts and I had not heard from him for some time. The last time that I heard from him he was not well, and I knew that he was so great for working that I feared he would break down.

So I wrote to Mrs. Wamsley, his daughter, and shall wait to hear how he is, for I know she will let me know at once as she is there with her father.

I have heard from her and he is better, thank God, and not dead, as so many thought, for he does so much work that no one thought that he could get over it.

And here on this 20th day of January I fell sick myself and have not been able to take up my work until the 4th day of March, and once more in the strength of the Lord I have taken up this work and hope to push it as fast I can, and I hope to finish it in the near future if the Lord wills. I hope that all who will may have the pleasure of knowing of something of the joys and of the sorrows that have crowned this little life of mine, but in and through it all I have seen the blessed hand of Him who is wise.

March 4th, 1897.